J
McH

McHugh, Fiona.

The Anne of Green
Gables storybook.

$16.95

DATE			
JUN 5 1991 8 -23			
7.23 Oct 21/93			
9-5 12/1			
AUG 11 1992 APR 1 3 1994			
SEP 0 8 1992 APR 2 7 1994			
SEP 2 8 1992 AUG 2 9 1994			
Oct 26 9-31			
DEC 1 5 1992 11/26			
JAN 0 5 1993			
JAN 1 9 1993			
FEB 1 0 1993			
MAR 0 3 1993			

The Anne of Green Gables Storybook

THE
Anne of Green Gables
STORYBOOK

based on
THE KEVIN SULLIVAN FILM
of
LUCY MAUD MONTGOMERY'S CLASSIC NOVEL

Screenplay by
KEVIN SULLIVAN & JOE WIESENFELD

Storybook adapted by
FIONA McHUGH

Firefly Books

Text adaptation: Fiona McHugh
Book design: Michael Solomon
Cover photography: William McLeod
Still photography: Rob McEwan, Rene Ohashi
Printed in Canada by D.W. Friesen Ltd.

Firefly Books Ltd
3520 Pharmacy Avenue, Unit 1-C
Scarborough, Ontario, Canada
M1W 2T8

MAY 8 '91

Canadian Cataloguing in Publication Data

McHugh, Fiona.
    The Anne of Green Gables storybook

ISBN 0-920668-43-7 (bound). – ISBN 0-920668-42-9 (pbk.)

I. Montgomery, L.M. (Lucy Maud), 1874–1942.   Anne of
Green Gables. II. Title.

PS8575.H8A8 1987   jC813'.54   C87-094696-X
PZ7.M35An   1987

There she weaves by night and day
A magic web with colours gay.
She has heard a whisper say,
A curse is on her if she stay
To look down to Camelot . . .

A NNE recited the lines slowly. The words hovered like bubbles in the bright air:

Willows whiten, aspens quiver
Little breezes dusk and shiver. . . .

It was a clear November morning in Marysville, Nova Scotia, and Anne Shirley was on her way back to the Hammond homestead with enough eggs and milk to feed the eight Hammond children. Keeping her eyes on her book, she shifted the basket of eggs to her other arm and struggled on up the hill. The full pail of milk banged against her side as she walked. A small white wave splashed over the rim and seeped down her skirt; but she paid no attention. In her imagination, she was no longer a skinny, red-haired orphan, but the beautiful and mysterious Lady of

Shalott. Tennyson's words had a magical ring. She spoke them aloud like a spell:

> There she weaves by night and day
> A magic web with colours gay.
> She has heard a whisper say,
> A curse is on her if she stay
> To look down to Camelot. . . .

A grating call carried up from the other side of the hill, shattering the dream:

"Anne! Anne Shirley! Get down here this minute! These twins need changin'. You're late with the eggs and milk! And Mr. Hammond's been waitin' a good hour for you to bring him his lunch!"

The Lady of Shallot vanished and plain Anne Shirley came down to earth with a bump. She was thirteen. She worked for nagging Mrs. Hammond, and she was behind with her chores!

By the time Anne arrived back at the cabin, Mrs. Hammond had worked herself into a fury. Dumping one of her damp babies into Anne's arms, she seized the precious book of poetry and flung it into the fire.

"I'll thank you to look after my babies, instead of porin' over them fool books o' yours," she snapped.

"I do enjoy babies in moderation, Mrs. Hammond," replied Anne, fighting back tears, "but twins three times in succession is too much. Besides," she added, trying not to watch as the Lady of Shalott went up in flames, "I simply couldn't live here if I didn't have any imagination."

Mrs. Hammond's eyes narrowed.

"I'll take none o' your cheek, Anne Shirley. One more word and it's back to the orphanage with you! Now get those babies changed before you take Mr. Hammond his lunch. And be quick about it or he'll give you a whippin' you won't forget."

Anne *meant* to hurry with Mr. Hammond's lunch, but she couldn't help noticing how the birches in the woods shone as golden as the sun. Then too there were heaps of leaves in the hollows and they rustled underfoot with such a satisfying sound,

they reminded her of poetry. She tried to keep from thinking about the Lady of Shalott, but it was hard not to mourn her. "I just love poetry that gives you that crinkly feeling up and down your back," she confided to a crimson maple.

As soon as she reached the mill, all thoughts of Ladies and poems were driven from Anne's mind. For Mr. Hammond had suffered a heart attack. In a fit of anger, he had run toward one of his employees, intending to strike him. But his own heart had struck the first blow. There he lay, stretched out and still—the last victim of his legendary bad temper.

Late that night, after she had put the children to bed, Anne spoke into the darkened mirror. "Katie," she whispered, "If only I hadn't lost myself in the beauty of the day, the one beauty which is allowed me, perhaps Mr. Hammond might still be with us." But even Katie, her imaginary friend, was silent.

Indeed, the shock of Mr. Hammond's death seemed to blanket the whole house in silence. The only sound was an occasional sniff from the grieving Mrs. Hammond, and the murmurings of her cousin, Essie, who had come to help with the funeral. Tiptoeing downstairs, Anne was arrested in mid-step by a sudden comment from Essie.

"That home girl," she said, and though her voice was quiet, it cut through Anne like a blade, "she'll have to go back where she came from."

Anne crept down the rest of the stairs and into the kitchen.

Mrs. Hammond sat at the table, staring bleakly into space. Essie stood behind her.

"Mrs. Hammond," faltered Anne. "Mrs. Hammond, I blame myself entirely for poor Mr. Hammond's death. To have to wait an extra hour for lunch is a terrible burden to place on any man. I shall never overcome my grief. But please, please don't send me back to the orphanage."

Mrs. Hammond's eyes seemed to look right through Anne.

"Orphan children are all the same," announced Essie to no one in particular, "Trash. That's what they are." Mrs. Hammond nodded. Her eyes slowly focussed on Anne. They were cold and empty. "Trash," she repeated dully, "That's right, Anne Shirley. I was daft when I took you in. I'd be daft to keep you!"

Anne backed out of the room, closing the door behind her. She stood alone in the shadowy hall, frightened by her own future.

It was the end of another long, uneventful day at the Fairview Orphanage in Hopetown. Amidst the flurry of bedtime preparations no one seemed to notice a still figure pressed against the window pane. Six months had passed since Mrs. Hammond returned a weeping Anne to the orphanage. During those six months, the only comfort the lonely child could find had lain in her imaginary world. "Katie," she whispered now, "I'm truly glad we have each other. It's so difficult finding a kindred spirit these days."

As she spoke, a tall figure entered the darkened dormitory. It was the director of the orphanage, Mrs. Cadbury. "Anne Shirley," she chided gently, "I might have known I'd find you here in the window seat instead of in your bed like everyone else."

"I'm sorry, Mrs. Cadbury," said Anne. "I don't mean to be difficult, truly I don't. It's just that my life is a perfect graveyard of buried hopes."

"Well then, perhaps my news may resurrect some of them," said Mrs. Cadbury, with a trace of a smile. "We've had a request for two of our girls to live with families in Prince Edward Island. And I intend that you shall be one of them."

The child's eyes glowed. "A family for me? Oh thank you, Mrs. Cadbury, thank you with all my heart."

Mrs. Rachel Lynde lived just where the Avonlea main road dipped down into a little hollow. It was a perfect setting for someone who was known throughout the length and breadth of Avonlea for her awesome ability to manage other peoples' concerns almost as well as her own. One afternoon in early June, she was sitting in her usual position on the front porch, when her sharp eye spotted something that almost made her drop her knitting. Could it be? Why, yes it was. It *was* Matthew Cuthbert driving that horse and buggy. And he was dressed in his best suit. Now where was Matthew Cuthbert going and why was he going there?

"I declare, I'm clean puzzled," she muttered, standing up to get a better look. "He's not going fast enough for the doctor. He's wearing his suit; so, he can't be going for turnip seed. Oh, my afternoon is ruined. I won't have a moment's peace until I know what that man is up to. Marilla is simply going to have to explain all this!"

Pausing only to skewer her hat to her head, she set out for Green Gables, the rambling, green and white house, where Marilla Cuthbert lived with her brother, Matthew.

As Mrs. Rachel stepped into Marilla's spotless kitchen, she noticed that the table was laid for three. Marilla must be expecting someone home with Matthew to tea. But who could it possibly be? Mrs. Rachel was dizzy with puzzlement.

"I was kind of worried about you, Marilla, when I saw your brother drive by just now. *In his suit.*"

Marilla looked like a woman of narrow experience and rigid conscience, which she was. But there was a saving something about her mouth that if it had been developed, might have hinted at a sense of humour. This afternoon her stern face held no clue to the mystery. Her whole attention seemed concentrated on the silver she was cleaning.

"I'm fine. Just fine, thank you, Rachel," she answered calmly.

Mrs. Rachel tapped her toes. Her elbows jerked with impatience.

"Matthew never goes to town this time of year, Marilla."

Marilla's tone gave nothing away. "Matthew wasn't going to town," she said evenly.

"Oh . . . Don't keep me in such suspense, for Heaven's sake!" implored Mrs. Rachel.

The tight lines around Marilla's mouth relented into a tiny smile. "He was going to Bright River," she explained. "We're getting a little boy from the orphanage at Hopetown. Matthew's gone to fetch him from the station."

If Marilla had said that Matthew had gone to Bright River to meet a kangaroo from Australia, Mrs. Rachel could not have been more astonished. She was actually stricken dumb for five seconds. "Why Marilla!" she exclaimed, when her voice finally returned to her, "A boy! Why you don't know the first thing about raising children! Whatever put such an idea into your head?"

Well, Matthew's getting along in years. He's not as spry as he once was. And his heart bothers him a good deal. Mrs. Spencer was up here a while back and she said she was getting a girl from Hopetown Asylum in the spring. Matthew and I thought it over and we decided to send word by Mrs. Spencer's niece, Roberta, to tell her to bring us home a boy while she was at it."

It was unavoidably clear to Mrs. Rachel that all this planning had taken place without benefit of her advice. Yet Marilla was calmly making tea and talking as if boys were fetched from asylums every day of the week!

"We told her to fix us up with a little boy of eleven or twelve," she was saying. "Old enough to do the chores and young enough to be brought up properly."

It was all too much for Mrs. Rachel. "Now look here," she burst out. "You know I pride myself on always speaking my mind. I'll just tell you plain that I think you're doing a mighty foolish thing. If you had asked my advice in the matter—which you didn't do, Marilla—I could have told you that what you're planning is risky. Why just last week I read in the paper how a couple took a boy out of an orphan asylum and he set fire to their house at night. *On purpose*! Burnt them to a crisp in their beds!"

"Well, I won't say that I haven't had my qualms, Rachel. But Matthew was real determined," replied Marilla, "and it's so seldom he sets his mind on anything that I felt I had to give in."

"And there was another case six months ago over in New Brunswick," broke in Mrs. Rachel eagerly, warming to her theme, "where an asylum child put strychnine in the well! The entire family died in agony. Only it was a girl in that instance."

"Well," said Marilla firmly, "We are not getting a girl."

When Matthew Cuthbert reached Bright River station, there was no sign of any train. He tied his horse in the yard and went to find the station master.

"Is the afternoon train due soon, Angus?" he enquired.

"Been and gone a half hour ago, Matthew" replied the stationmaster. "There was a passenger dropped off for you. She's waiting out there on the platform. I told her she could wait in the ladies' waiting room. But she said there was more scope for her imagination outside."

"She?" echoed Matthew hoarsely. "But it's a boy I came for!"

"Well I dare say she can explain it all," said the stationmaster, chuckling. "That one has a tongue of her own."

Matthew Cuthbert's shyness was legendary. He dreaded all women except his sister, Marilla. His first instinct was to get back in the buggy and drive away as fast as he could. But instead he groaned inwardly and peered cautiously around the edge of the building. There was no boy in sight. Only a thin, red-headed girl clutching a shabby carpetbag. Matthew gulped. She was gazing straight at him. She was bounding toward him. In a second, Matthew was staring down into a face that was small, white, and thin. It was also much-freckled. The eyes that smiled up at him looked sometimes green, sometimes grey.

"I suppose you are Mr. Matthew Cuthbert of Green Gables?" she said, in a voice that was peculiarly clear and sweet. "I'm very glad to see you. I was beginning to be afraid you weren't coming for me tonight. I had made up my mind to climb up that big wild cherry tree and wait for you there till morning. It would be lovely to sleep in a cherry tree all white with bloom in the moonshine, don't you think?"

"Oh . . . yes, it would. I mean no, it wouldn't. I mean . . . " said Matthew in agony, "there's been a big mistake."

"Oh no, there's no mistake," the mysterious creature assured

"I've always heard that Prince Edward Island was the prettiest spot in Canada."

him earnestly, "Not if you're Mr. Matthew Cuthbert. Mrs. Spencer told me to wait right here for you and so I've done. Most pleasantly, I must say. This is beautiful country you have here, Mr. Cuthbert."

She was holding out her hand to him. Matthew took it awkwardly in his. There and then he decided what to do. He could not tell this child with the glowing eyes that there had been a mistake. He would take her home and let Marilla do that.

"I'm sorry I was late," he said shyly. "Come along. The horse is in the yard."

Once in the buggy, the child could barely contain her delight. "Oh, it seems so wonderful that I'm going to live with you and belong to you," she burst out. "I've never belonged to anybody before. And the asylum was the worst place I've lived in yet. I don't suppose you were ever an orphan in an asylum so you can't possibly understand what it's like. It's worse than anything you can imagine. Mrs. Spencer says it's wicked of me to talk like that. But I don't mean to be wicked. It's just so easy to be wicked without knowing it, isn't it?"

Matthew, much to his own surprise, was enjoying himself in the company of this freckled witch. He thought that he kind of liked her chatter.

"Why look," she was saying, "there are some more cherry trees in bloom. This island is the bloomiest place. I just love it already. I've always heard that Prince Edward Island was the prettiest spot in Canada, and I used to dream I was living here. This is the first dream that's ever come true for me."

She looked over at Matthew. "You know, just now I feel pretty nearly perfectly happy. I can't feel *exactly* perfectly happy because . . . well, what colour would you call this?" She twitched one of her long glossy braids over her thin shoulder and held it up before Matthew's eyes.

Matthew was not used to deciding on the tints of ladies' tresses, but in this case there couldn't be much doubt.

"It's red, ain't it?"

The girl's sigh seemed to come from her very toes. "Yes, it's red," she said sadly. "Now you see why I can't be perfectly happy. I know I'm skinny and a little freckled and my eyes are green. But I can imagine I have a beautiful rose petal complexion and lovely starry violet eyes. But I cannot imagine my red hair away. It will be my lifelong sorrow. Have you ever imagined what it must feel like to be divinely beautiful?"

Matthew swallowed. "Well now, no, I haven't . . . " he confessed.

"I have, often. Which would you rather be: divinely beautiful or dazzlingly clever or angelically good?"

Matthew was beginning to feel as he had once felt in his youth, when another boy had coaxed him onto the merry-go-round at a picnic. "Well now . . . I dunno exactly."

"Neither do I. I know I'll never be angelically good. Mrs. Spencer says I talk too much and — Oh, Mr. Cuthbert! Oh, Mr. Cuthbert! Oh, Mr. Cuthbert!"

That was not what Mrs. Spencer had said, nor had Matthew done anything astonishing. They had simply rounded a curve

and found themselves in a stretch of road completely arched over with huge, wide-spreading apple trees. Overhead was one long canopy of snowy fragrant bloom. Below the boughs, the air was full of a purple twilight. Its beauty seemed to strike the child dumb. She leaned back in the buggy, her face lifted rapturously to the white splendour above.

Matthew glanced over at her. "Pretty, ain't it? Folks call it the Avenue."

"Pretty doesn't seem the right word to use. Nor beautiful either. It's the first thing I ever saw that couldn't be improved on by imagination. It gave me a queer funny ache and yet it was a pleasant ache. Did you ever have an ache like that, Mr. Cuthbert?"

"Well now, I just can't recollect that I ever had."

"I have it whenever I see anything royally beautiful. But they shouldn't call this place the Avenue. They should call it . . . " she paused, "the White Way of Delight."

They turned out of the Avenue and drove over the crest of a hill. Below them was a pond, its water a glory of many shifting hues. On a slope beyond, a little grey house peered around a white apple orchard.

"That's Barry's pond," said Matthew.

"I shall call it the Lake of Shining Waters. I know that's the right name for it, because whenever I hit on a name that suits exactly, it gives me a thrill. Do things ever give you a thrill, Mr. Cuthbert?"

Matthew ruminated. "Well now, yes. Digging up them ugly white grubs in the cucumber beds."

Anne smiled and tucked her arm inside his. They had reached the crest of a hill. To the west, a dark church spire rose up against a marigold sky. Below was a little valley where, far back from the road, stood a farmstead, dimly white with blossoming trees in the twilight of the surrounding woods.

"There," said Matthew, pointing proudly, "Yonder's Green Gables."

Anne gazed at it rapturously. "Just as soon as I saw it I felt it was home. Oh, it seems as if I must be in a dream. I've pinched myself so many times today to make sure that all this was real. But it *is* real. And we're nearly home."

Marilla came briskly forward as Matthew entered the hall. But she stopped short when her eyes fell on the odd little figure clutching the faded carpetbag.

"Matthew Cuthbert," she demanded, "who is that?"

"It's a girl," answered Matthew wretchedly.

"I can see that. Where is the boy?"

"There weren't any. Just her," replied Matthew, staring at the carpet. "I figured we just couldn't leave her there, no matter what the mistake was."

"Well," said Marilla, almost speechless, "this is a fine kettle of fish! This is what comes of sending word instead of going ourselves."

All the animation faded from Anne's face. Suddenly she seemed to grasp the full meaning of what was being said.

"You don't want me!" she cried. "You don't want me because I'm not a boy! Nobody ever did want me. I might have known this was all too beautiful to be true!" She burst into tears.

Matthew and Marilla stared at each other over her bent head. Neither of them knew what to say or do. Finally Marilla spoke. "Come now," she said awkwardly. "Don't cry so. It isn't your fault."

"Oh," sobbed the child, "this is the most tragical thing that ever happened to me."

Something like a reluctant smile, rusty from long disuse, softened Marilla's grim expression. "What's your name, child?" she asked.

"Would you please call me Cordelia?"

"*Call* you Cordelia! Is that your name?"

"It's not exactly my name. But I would love to be called Cordelia. It's such a perfectly elegant name."

"What is your name child, and no more nonsense."

"What's your name, child?"

"Anne Shirley," answered the owner of that name reluctantly. "Plain old unromantic Anne Shirley."

"Unromantic fiddlesticks!" said the unsympathetic Marilla. "Anne Shirley is a fine sensible name and hardly one to be ashamed of."

"Oh, I'm not ashamed of it," explained Anne. "But if you must call me Anne, would you please be sure to spell it with an **e**. Anne with an **e** looks quite distinguished. So if you'll only call me Anne with an **e**, I shall try to reconcile myself to not being called Cordelia."

"Very well then, Anne with an **e**," said Marilla in exasperation, "How is it that *you* happened to be picked instead of a boy?"

"If I were very beautiful and had nut-brown hair, would you keep me?"

"No," said Marilla firmly. "We want a boy to help Matthew on the farm. A girl would be of no use to us. Now bring your bag and come along upstairs. We'll have to put you somewhere for the night."

Later that evening, Marilla spoke her mind to Matthew.

"I'm taking her over to that Spencer woman in the morning. She'll have to be sent back to the asylum."

"I suppose," said Matthew reluctantly.

"You suppose! Don't you know it?"

"She's a real interesting little thing, Marilla. Seems a pity to send her back. She's so set on staying."

Marilla's astonishment knew no bounds. "Matthew Cuthbert, I believe that child has bewitched you! I can see as plain as plain you want to keep her."

"We could hire a boy to help me," said Matthew, "and she'd be company for you."

"I'm not suffering for company," replied Marilla shortly. "Particularly not for someone who prattles on without stopping for breath. She'll have to go straight back where she came from. What good would she be to us?"

"We might be some good to *her*," said Matthew suddenly and unexpectedly.

After she had put her dishes away, Marilla went to bed, frowning most resolutely. And upstairs, in the east gable, a lonely, friendless child cried herself to sleep.

The next morning Matthew reluctantly hitched the sorrel mare into the buggy and helped Marilla and Anne up. "Little Jerry Buote from the Creek was around," he said to Marilla, "and I told him I guessed I'd hire him for the summer." Marilla made no reply, but she hit the unlucky sorrel such a vicious clip with the whip that the fat mare, unused to such treatment, whizzed indignantly down the lane at an alarming pace. Looking back once, Marilla saw her brother leaning over the gate, looking wistfully after them.

Mrs. Spencer lived in a big yellow house at White Sands Cove. She and her daughter, Flora Jane, came running down the front steps as Marilla drove the buggy up to the door. Surprise and welcome mingled on Mrs. Spencer's kindly face.

"Why, Marilla," she exclaimed, "you're the last person I expected to see today. I imagined you'd be getting Anne settled. And how are you, Anne?"

A blight seemed to have descended on Anne. "I'm as well as a victim of tragic circumstances could be, thank you," she replied tonelessly.

"The fact is, there's been some queer mistake, Sarah," explained Marilla. "We told Roberta for you to get us a boy."

"Marilla Cuthbert, you don't say so!" gasped Mrs. Spencer, "Why Roberta distinctly said you wanted a girl."

"I suppose the asylum will take the child back?" asked Marilla.

"Well, as a matter of fact Mrs. Blewett was up here yesterday, asking me if I could get her a little girl. She has ten children you know and another on the way. Anne would be just the kind of help she needs."

"Excuse me, Mrs. Spencer," interrupted Anne in mortal dread,

"But you're wiry and I don't know but the wiry ones can work the hardest."

"But would there happen to be any twins among them?"

"Why she has two sets of twins," replied Mrs. Spencer. "How did you know, child?"

"Twins seem to be my lot in life," said Anne mournfully.

Just then a shrill voice hailed Mrs. Spencer and she turned in astonishment. "I declare, if that isn't Mrs. Blewett coming up the lane this blessed minute!" she exclaimed, "Why I call this positively providential."

Mrs. Blewett was a shrewish-faced woman without an ounce of spare flesh on her bones. She greeted the group coldly.

"Mrs. Blewett, this is Anne Shirley," beamed Mrs. Spencer, "I think she'll be just the thing for you."

Mrs. Blewett's sharp eyes darted over Anne from head to foot. "How old are you, girl?" she demanded.

"Thirteen," whispered Anne.

"Humph!" sniffed Mrs. Blewett, "Ain't much to you. But you're wiry and I don't know but the wiry ones can work the hardest. I'll expect you to earn your keep. And I want you to act smart and be respectful." She turned toward Marilla. "I'll take her off your hands this minute, Miss Cuthbert," she announced virtuously. "My twins are awful fractious these days and I'm clean worn out."

But Marilla had been watching Anne. She had seen in the pale face such a look of misery, that she felt moved to help.

"Well now, I don't know," she said slowly. "Perhaps I oughtn't to make a decision until I speak to Matthew. I'll just take her home again and consult him. Good afternoon, ladies." With that Marilla cracked the whip and the buggy moved off down the lane.

A faint flush of hope crept up Anne's cheeks. "Oh, Miss Cuthbert," she whispered, as if speaking aloud might shatter the glorious possibility, "Did you really say it or did I only just imagine it?"

"I haven't said anything yet, young lady," retorted Marilla sharply. "Sending you back to the orphanage is one thing. Handing you over to the likes of Mathilda Blewett is another. And if you can't distinguish between what is real and what isn't, I think you'd better learn to control that imagination of yours."

Anne folded her hands meekly. "I'll try to do anything and be anything you want, Miss Cuthbert," she said, "if only you'll keep me."

When they returned to Green Gables, Matthew met them in the lane. Marilla could read the relief in his face when he saw that she had at least brought Anne back with her. But she said nothing until later when she went out to the barn to talk things over with him.

"I wouldn't give a dog I liked to that Blewett woman," she announced defensively. Matthew continued milking the cows. He remained silent.

"It makes no sense to keep her," floundered Marilla, "No sense at all." Matthew made no reply.

"But . . . " continued Marilla, all in a rush, "But if we *did* keep her, I'd expect you not to interfere with my methods. An old maid like me may not know much about raising a child, but I know a darn sight more than an old bachelor like you." Matthew's face was a glow of delight. But he kept his eyes lowered and his mouth determinedly closed.

"I'll say one thing for her though," said Marilla with a dry chuckle, "She can talk the hind leg off a mule. And won't that be a nice change around here!"

When Anne came down to breakfast the next morning, she confronted Marilla with the air of one determined to know the worst. "Oh please, Miss Cuthbert," she implored, "Tell me if you're going to send me back. I just can't bear not knowing any longer."

"Well, you'll just have to bear it," said Marilla, "because I simply don't know. I thought maybe we'd put it on trial for a while. For all our sakes. Would that suit you?"

"If you think it's necessary, Miss Cuthbert," replied Anne, sitting down at the table.

"One thing I will insist on though," continued Marilla, "is

that while you're under my roof you will say your prayers. So here." She thrust an illustrated card under Anne's nose. "Learn that while you're eating your breakfast."

"Our father, who art in Heaven." read Anne aloud, "Hallowed be Thy name . . . why, Miss Cuthbert," she broke off delightedly, "It's just like a line of music. I'm so glad you thought of making me learn this."

"Well learn it, then, and hold your tongue," said Marilla in exasperation. She had just spied Rachel Lynde bustling up the garden path and was not sure she felt capable of coping with that lady's inspection of Anne.

"Can't you send her back, Marilla?" was the question uttered by Mrs. Rachel almost as soon as she had crossed the threshold. For she had been one of the first in Avonlea to hear about what she termed 'Marilla's mistake.'

"We're . . . we're still considering on it," replied Marilla uncertainly.

"Considering . . . What is there to consider?" demanded Mrs. Rachel. "Lawful heart!" she continued, as Anne stood up to be introduced. "Her looks are certainly nothing to consider. Did anyone ever see such freckles! She's terrible skinny and homely, Marilla. And her hair is as red as carrots!"

With one bound Anne crossed the kitchen floor and stood before Mrs. Rachel. Her lips quivered. Her face was scarlet with anger. "How dare you!" she cried in a voice choked with rage. "How dare you call me skinny and ugly? How dare you call me freckled and red headed? You're a rude, unfeeling woman, and I'll never forgive you, never, never!"

"Anne Shirley!" exclaimed Marilla.

But Anne, head up, eyes blazing, continued to face Mrs. Lynde. "How would you like to have nasty things said about you?" she stormed. "How would you like to be told that you're fat and ugly and a sour old gossip and probably hadn't a spark of imagination in you?"

"Anne!" called Marilla sharply. But it was too late. Anne had rushed from the house, slamming the door behind her.

"You mark my words, Marilla," declared Mrs. Rachel darkly, "that's the kind puts strychnine in the well." Clutching her tattered dignity, she swept toward the door. "Goodbye, Marilla. Come down and see me when you can. But don't expect me to visit here ever again, if I'm to be treated in such a fashion." And with an air of offended majesty, Mrs. Rachel waddled from the house.

Marilla found Anne in the garden, face down on a bench, sobbing her heart out. "Anne Shirley," she said angrily, "when I said 'trial', I never thought you'd take me literally. You had no right to speak to Mrs. Lynde in that way."

"She had no right to say what she did" wailed Anne, her face swollen and tear-stained.

Alarmed by the slamming of doors and the abrupt departure of Mrs. Rachel, Matthew had approached the house from the vegetable patch, where he had been working. Now, seeing Marilla in close discussion with a weeping Anne, he paused. Unwilling to interfere, he was too unsettled by Anne's evident distress to return to work.

"Rachel deserves an apology and you will go to her and give it," he heard Marilla declare firmly.

"Oh Miss Cuthbert," sobbed Anne, "I can never do that. You can shut me up in a dark, damp dungeon inhabited by snakes and toads and feed me only on bread and water and I won't complain. But I cannot ask Mrs. Lynde to forgive me."

"We're not in the habit of shutting people up in dark, damp dungeons," said Marilla drily, "especially as they're rather scarce in Avonlea. But apologize to Mrs. Lynde you must and shall."

"How can I tell Mrs. Lynde I'm sorry when I'm not? I'm sorry I've vexed you. But I'm *glad* I said those things to her. I can't even *imagine* I'm sorry."

"If you expect to remain under my roof," said Marilla, and her tone was final, "you will apologize to Mrs. Lynde."

Matthew watched uncomfortably as Anne straightened her shoulders and looked straight into Marilla's eyes.

"That's the kind puts strychnine in the well."

"Then you'll have to send me back," she said quietly.
Marilla rose to her feet. She felt very old all of a sudden.
"Very well then, Anne. Go to your room."

Matthew waited until Marilla went out that evening to bring the cows from the back pasture. Then, with the air of a burglar, he slipped into the house and crept upstairs. Anne was sitting by the window. Her carpetbag waited at her feet.

"Ain't been upstairs in this house in four years," said Matthew shyly. Anne's red eyes and tear-stained face touched his heart.

"I guess you're leavin' then." he said sadly.

"Oh Matthew, I'd rather die than apologize to Mrs. Lynde."

Matthew shifted uneasily. "Well now, Marilla's a dreadful determined woman — dreadful determined. You don't have to be *exactly* sorry, you know. You can be sorta sorry."

"But I'm not sorry at all," objected Anne.

"I hear Mrs. Blewett's an awful workhorse. Besides, Anne, it'd be awful lonesome around here without you. Couldn't you just smooth it over?"

Anne studied Matthew's face. "You mean," she said slowly, "you mean, you really don't want me to go?"

Matthew shook his head. This discovery seemed to inspire Anne.

"Why Matthew, I'd do anything for you. If you really don't want me to go, why then it certainly wouldn't be right to let Mrs. Lynde be the cause of our parting. I don't — as you say — have to be exactly sorry. I just have to remove the disgrace I've brought to Marilla's good name."

"That's right — that's right, Anne," said Matthew, eagerly. "Just smooth it over so to speak. That's what I was trying to get at." He patted her head gently. "Don't tell Marilla I said anything, will you? She'll say I'm interferin'."

"Wild horses couldn't drag it from me," promised Anne solemnly.

Smiling, Matthew tiptoed from the room, a little frightened by his own success.

Upon her return to the house, Marilla was agreeably surprised to see a penitent Anne enter the kitchen. "I'm sorry I lost my temper and said those rude things, Miss Cuthbert," she said meekly, "and I'm willing to go and tell Mrs. Lynde so."

"Very well." Marilla's crispness gave no sign of her relief. She had spent the last few hours agonizing over what she should do if Anne did not give in. "I'll take you over first thing. Now get up to bed and don't forget to say your prayers."

After Anne had skipped off to bed, Marilla turned to her brother. "I knew she'd come to her senses if we left her alone," she said loftily. Matthew merely nodded and continued drinking his tea.

Mrs. Rachel Lynde was sitting in her usual observation post on the front porch when Marilla arrived with Anne in tow the next morning. Before a word could be spoken, Anne fell to her knees in front of the astonished Rachel.

"Oh, Mrs. Lynde, I am so extremely sorry," she said with a quiver in her voice; "I have disgraced my good friends who have let me stay at Green Gables even though I am not a boy. What you said was true. I am skinny and ugly and my hair is red. What I said about you was true too, only I shouldn't have said it. Please, Mrs. Lynde, please forgive me. You wouldn't be so cruel as to inflict a lifelong sorrow on a poor orphan, would you? Please say you forgive me!"

All resentment vanished from Mrs. Lynde's kindly, if officious, heart.

"There, there, child," she said warmly, "of course I forgive you. You mustn't mind me. I'm known throughout these parts as a woman who speaks her mind. And don't worry about your hair. I knew a girl once who had hair every bit as red as yours. But when she grew up it darkened into a real handsome auburn."

Anne drew a deep breath as she rose to her feet. "You have given me hope, Mrs. Lynde," she said, "I shall always think of you as a benefactor."

"Don't you ever imagine things differently from what they are?"

"Laws, Marilla," said Rachel, strangely satisfied, "all this child needs is discipline and a proper education. The Sunday School picnic's scheduled this week for Barry's field. I want you to take Anne so she can meet some civilized children her own age. And trial or no trial, you ought to put her in school."

As Marilla and Anne walked home from Rachel's, Marilla brought up the subject of school once more. "Putting you in school doesn't mean I've come to a decision, Anne. It's just as easy to take you out as put you in."

"It does give a person room to hope, though, Miss Cuthbert. Besides, my temper will never get the better of me again, I promise."

"I hope not," said Marilla fervently. "Good behaviour in the first place is more important than theatrical apologies afterward."

"I thought since I had to do it, I might as well do it thoroughly."

"Save your thoroughness for prayer, Anne. God does not want a fair-weather friend."

"The only real friend I ever had was Katie Maurice," said Anne mournfully, "and she was really just my window friend."

"Window friend?"

"I discovered her in the window of Mrs. Thomas' bookcase. It was the only window which hadn't been smashed by her intoxicated husband. I lived with the Thomases before I lived with the Hammonds. I used to wish I knew the spell to step through the glass into Katie's world which was so beautiful."

"Well I don't think you should have window friends anymore, Anne," said Marilla shortly. For a while they walked on in silence. Then Anne spoke again. "Do you think I shall ever have a bosom friend, Miss Cuthbert?" she asked.

"A . . . a what kind of friend?"

"A bosom friend. A really kindred spirit. I've dreamt of meeting her all my life."

"Diana Barry lives over there on Orchard Slope," Marilla pointed. "She's about your age. Her parents are sponsoring the picnic next Sunday. You can meet her then."

"Diana," murmured Anne dreamily. "Diana of the Lake of Shining Waters."

"For mercy's sake, child, you set your heart too much on silly names."

"What name should I call you, Miss Cuthbert?" asked Anne. "May I call you Aunt Marilla?"

"You can call me just plain Marilla," said Marilla sternly. "I don't believe in calling people names that are not their own."

"Couldn't you imagine that you were my aunt?"

"No, I could not."

"Don't you ever imagine things differently from what they are?"

"No, I do not."

"Oh, Marilla," sighed Anne, slipping her hand into the older woman's hard palm, "how much you miss!"

Something warm and pleasant welled up in Marilla's heart at the touch of that thin little hand in hers. Perhaps it was a throb of the maternity she had missed, but it caused a glow of happiness that surprised her.

"No, I do not."

From then on, Anne thought picnic and talked picnic and dreamed picnic. But several days before the charmed event was to take place, Marilla came downstairs with a troubled face.

"Anne," she said, "Have you touched my amethyst brooch? I thought I stuck it in my pincushion when I came home from church, but I can't find it anywhere."

"I . . . I did touch it," admitted Anne. "It's such a perfectly elegant brooch. I pinned it on yesterday, just for a minute. Amethysts are my idea of what diamonds should be like, Marilla. I think those lovely purple stones must be the souls of good violets, don't you?"

But Marilla was in no mood for fanciful speculation. "You had no right to meddle with my things, Anne. That brooch isn't anywhere on the bureau. You can't have put it back."

"I did put it back," said Anne quickly—pertly, Marilla

thought. "I just don't remember whether I stuck it on the pin-cushion or laid it in the china tray. But I'm perfectly certain I put it back."

"I'll go and have another look," said Marilla, determined to be just. "If you put that brooch back, it's there still. If it isn't, I'll know you didn't."

Marilla returned to her room and made a thorough search, not only over the bureau but in every other place she thought the brooch might possibly be. It was not to be found.

"Anne," she said, re-entering the kitchen, "the brooch is gone. By your own admission, you were the last person to handle it. Now what have you done with it. Tell me the truth at once. Did you take it out and lose it?"

"No, I didn't," said Anne, meeting Marilla's gaze squarely. "I never took the brooch out of your room and that's the truth, if I was to be led to the block for it — although I'm not very certain what a block is. So there, Marilla."

Anne's 'so there' was only intended to emphasize what she had said, but Marilla took it as a display of defiance.

"I believe you are telling me a falsehood, Anne," she said sharply. "Go to your room and stay there until you are ready to confess."

"You *will* let me out for the picnic, won't you?" asked Anne as she obediently left the room, "I just have to go to the picnic, Marilla."

"You're not going to the picnic or anywhere else until you tell me the truth."

"But if I don't go to the picnic, how will I ever make a bosom friend? Or any friend at all?"

"That brooch meant a great deal to me, Anne. More than any picnic. Now go to your room."

The next few days were troubled ones for Marilla. She emptied out drawers. She combed through every crack and cranny. But still no brooch appeared. And still Anne, confined to her room, refused to admit she had taken it.

"Now I realize I was right not to be too hasty about keeping her," said Marilla to Matthew. It was the Sunday of the picnic and she was in the kitchen, preparing breakfast.

"We can't keep a liar and a thief, and you know it, Matthew."

Matthew was confounded and puzzled. He had to admit that everything pointed to Anne as being the one who had taken the brooch, but he could not quickly lose faith in her.

When Marilla took Anne's breakfast up to her on a tray, she found the child sitting on the edge of the bed, looking pale and resolute.

"I'm ready to confess, Marilla."

Marilla put down the tray. She felt no sense of triumph. "Let me hear what you have to say then, Anne."

Somehow Anne sounded as if she were repeating a lesson she had learned. "I took the brooch," she said, "because I was overcome by an irresistible temptation. I was imagining I was Lady Cordelia Fitzgerald and I just had to wear the brooch as I trod the footbridge over the Lake of Shining Waters. I took the brooch off to admire how it shone in the sunlight. And then, as I leaned over the bridge, to gaze at my reflection in the lake, with the wind blowing my auburn hair, the brooch slipped from my fingers and sank, all purply-sparkling, beneath the rippling waves. And that's the best I can do at confessing. May I go to the picnic now?"

Marilla felt hot anger surge up in her heart. This child had taken and lost her treasured brooch and now sat there calmly reciting details, without the least show of repentance.

"You'll go to no picnic, Anne Shirley. You can pack your bags and start imagining life with Mrs. Blewett!" And so saying, Marilla slammed the door and stormed down the stairs to get ready for church.

"Rachel Lynde was right," she fumed to the waiting Matthew as she threw her shawl over her shoulders, "I should never have let that child worm her way into my affections."

"Marilla!" Matthew's doleful expression transformed into one of delight. "Oh, Marilla, look!" Something was caught in the strands of shawl, something that glittered and sparkled in facets of violet light.

Marilla snatched at it with a gasp. It was the amethyst brooch!

"Dear life and heart!" said Marilla blankly, "how can it be? Here's my brooch safe and sound that I thought was at the bottom of Barry's pond."

Brooch in hand, she rushed up the stairs and into Anne's room. "Whatever made you say you took it and lost it?" she demanded, holding out the brooch.

"You said you'd keep me in my room till I confessed," returned Anne wearily. "I simply *had* to go to the picnic and so I thought out a confession last night in bed, and made it as interesting as I could."

"But it was still a lie," objected Marilla.

"You wouldn't believe the truth," said Anne simply.

Marilla's conscience pricked her. "Anne, you do beat all! But I was wrong—I see that now. I shouldn't have doubted your word when I've never known you to tell a lie. Of course, it wasn't right to confess to a thing you hadn't done. But I drove you to it." She stretched out her hand to the child. "So if you'll forgive me, Anne, I'll forgive you and we'll start square again. Now get dressed for the service. And this afternoon we'll go to the picnic together."

She tasted ice-cream for the first time in her entire life.

That afternoon shone forever in Anne's memory with a golden light. She tasted ice-cream for the first time in her entire life, an experience she could only describe in one word: 'sublime'. But best of all, she met her longed-for bosom friend at last. Diana Barry was pretty enough to satisfy even Anne's beauty-starved heart. Her hair was thick and raven-dark, her cheeks were rosy, and her black eyes danced with merriment.

"She reads entirely too much," her mother complained to Marilla, as the two girls eyed each other shyly, "and I can't prevent her, for her father aids and abets her. I'm glad she has the prospect of a playmate. Perhaps it'll take her out-of-doors more."

Diana and Anne wandered down to the river in bashful

silence. When Anne finally spoke, it was almost in a whisper. "Diana," she asked timidly, "do you think you can like me enough to be my bosom friend?"

Diana laughed. Diana always laughed before she spoke. "Why, I guess so," she said frankly. "I'm awfully glad you've come to live at Green Gables, Anne. There isn't any other girl who lives near enough to play with, and I've no sisters big enough."

"Don't you think he's handsome?"

Anne let out a huge sigh of relief. She could feel happiness pouring into her heart.

"C'mon," she urged, taking Diana's hand, "we don't want to miss the races!"

Later on, tired out from running and chattering and laughing, they sat contentedly together by the water's edge and watched the boats gliding by.

"There's Mr. Phillips, our teacher," Diana pointed at a young man who was gazing soulfully at his boating companion. "You'll meet him when you start school. That's Prissy Andrews with him. He's helping her study for her entrance to Queen's. He's dead gone on her. Prissy's got a beautiful complexion and he moons over her something terrible."

Another boat floated by containing several giggling girls. One of them was leaning over the edge, trying to reach a water lily.

"That Josie Pye," commented Diana scornfully. "She's always looking for attention. 'Specially from Gilbert Blythe." Following Diana's gaze, Anne's eyes came to rest on a tall boy with curly brown hair sitting nearby on the bank.

"Don't you think he's handsome?" asked Diana, "Josie Pye certainly does."

Just then, the boat full of giggling girls tipped slightly and Josie fell into the water with a loud splash.

"I hope she nearly drowns," muttered Diana savagely.

"I wish it had been me," sighed Anne, carried away by the afternoon's excitement, "It must be such a romantic experience to nearly drown."

Diana burst out laughing. "What a strange girl you are, Anne Shirley! All the same, I can tell we're going to get along really well."

Anne's cup of happiness overflowed.

Anne's first morning at school started off well. Mr. Phillips made a note of her name and then directed her to share a seat with Diana.

It wasn't until Gilbert Blythe took it into his head to tease the new arrival that things began to go badly. Gilbert had been trying all morning — and failing utterly — to make Anne Shirley look at him. For Anne, with her chin propped on her hands and her eyes fixed on the blue glimpse of the Lake of Shining Waters that the west window afforded, was far away in a dreamland of her own. Gilbert Blythe wasn't used to putting himself out to make a girl look at him and meeting with failure. She *should* look at him, that red-haired Shirley girl with the pointed chin and the big eyes that weren't like the eyes of any other girl in Avonlea school. Reaching across the aisle, he picked up the end of one of Anne's long braids, held it at arm's length and hissed one word: "Carrots!"

Then Anne looked at him with a vengeance! She did more than look. She sprang to her feet. "You mean, hateful boy!" she cried, "How dare you!"

And then — Crack! She had picked up her slate and smacked it down on Gilbert's head with such force that the slate broke clean in two.

The whole class fell silent in horrified delight. In the sudden quiet, Mr. Phillips stalked down the aisle and laid his heavy hand on Anne's shoulder.

"Anne Shirley, what is the meaning of this?" he demanded.

Gilbert spoke up stoutly. "It was my fault, Mr. Phillips. I teased her."

"How dare you!"

Mr. Phillips paid no attention to Gilbert. Marching Anne to the front of the class, he wrote on the blackboard for all to see:

ANN SHIRLEY HAS A VERY BAD TEMPER.

Then he read it out loud, so that even the primer class, who couldn't read, should understand. "You will write this out 100 times before leaving today," he thundered.

With a white, set face Anne obeyed. But before beginning, she stood on tiptoe and added an **e** to the ANN that Mr. Phillips had inscribed on the board.

When school was dismissed, Anne marched out with her red head held high. Gilbert Blythe tried to intercept her at the porch door.

"I'm awfully sorry I made fun of your hair, Anne," he whispered contritely. "Honest I am. Don't be mad at me for keeps now."

Anne swept by disdainfully, without look or sign of hearing.

"Oh Anne, how could you?" breathed Diana as they walked down the lane together. Her tone was half-reproachful, half-admiring, for Diana felt that she could never have resisted Gilbert's plea. "Gilbert makes fun of all the girls," she said soothingly. "Why he calls me crow-head all the time—because my hair's so black—and I've never heard him apologize before either."

"There's a world of difference between being called crow-head and being called carrots," retorted Anne. "I shall never forgive Gilbert Blythe. The iron has entered my soul, Diana. My mind is made up. My red hair is a curse."

Just what Anne had meant when she said her mind was made up was left for Marilla to discover a short while later. Having heard from Rachel Lynde about Anne's disastrous day at school, Marilla had rushed upstairs to confront her troublesome charge. She found the bedroom door locked.

"Anne Shirley!" she called, rapping as hard as she could, "I've heard all about it. Now you open this door at once!"

"Please go away, Marilla," came the muffled response, "I am in the depths of despair!"

"Despair, fiddlesticks!" grumped Marilla, "You open this door immediately!"

Marilla heard the bolt slide reluctantly open. But before she could enter the room, Anne had scuttled back to bed, throwing the covers over herself so that she was completely hidden from view. In one long stride, Marilla reached the bed and jerked back the covers. What she saw made her freeze with shock.

"Anne Shirley," she gasped, "what have you done to your hair! Why, it's *green*!"

Green it most certainly was—a queer, dull, bronzy green, with streaks here and there of the original red to heighten the ghastly effect. Never in all her life had Marilla seen anything so grotesque as Anne's hair at that moment.

"Oh Marilla," wailed Anne, all crumpled up in the bed, "I thought nothing could be as bad as red hair. Green is ten times worse. You little know how utterly wretched I am."

"I little know how you got into this fix, but I demand that you tell me!"

"I dyed it," sobbed Anne. "He positively assured me it would turn a beautiful raven black!"

"Who did? Who are you talking about, child?"

"The peddler we met on the road today. Oh, Marilla, what shall I do? I'll never be able to live this down. I can't face him again. That Gilbert Blythe had no right to call me carrots!"

Marilla sat down on the bed beside the sobbing child.

"Did you really smash your slate over that boy's head?" she asked.

If Anne had looked up, she might have seen a slight smile hovering in Marilla's eyes. But Anne was too submerged in her own sorrow to notice. "I'm afraid I did," she gulped.

"Hard?" asked Marilla, and now the smile had definitely decided to stay.

"Very hard, yes." Anne blew her nose.

It was then that Marilla made up her mind. "I should be furious with you, Anne," she said softly, "your first day at school. What a way to behave. But . . . if you promise me that nothing

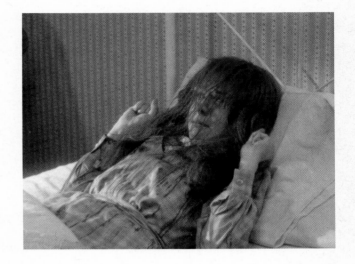

"You little know how utterly wretched I am."

of this sort will happen again, I won't say another word about it."

"You mean . . . you're not going to send me back?" asked Anne, unable to believe her ears.

Marilla smiled. "I've come to a decision," she said. "The trial is over, Anne. You will stay at Green Gables."

Anne sat bolt upright in bed, her green hair forgotten. She stared at Marilla as if trying to take in what she had said. "Stay at Green Gables . . . ." she repeated slowly. "Stay here with you and Matthew? Oh Marilla!" she flung her arms around her, "Do you mean I can really belong to you now?"

Marilla stood up, gently disengaging Anne's arms.

"Something tells me you do belong here, child, after all," she said as she left the room.

That evening, while Matthew drank his tea in the kitchen, Marilla skilfully cut Anne's hair. Wrapped in a sheet to protect her clothes, Anne surveyed the green curls lying at her feet. When Marilla had finished, Matthew shyly put his arm around Anne.

"You're our girl now," he said proudly, "and the prettiest one this side of Halifax."

As the months passed, Anne's hair grew back to its former length, only glossier and thicker. Her happiness grew too. She and Diana spent many happy hours together, racing along the sandy beaches, reading aloud to each other or simply talking quietly, as good friends do. Her confidence in school had also increased. By the time Spring came, she was doing almost as well as Gilbert Blythe. Mr. Phillips discovered this during their monthly spelling bee. "Miss Andrews," he said, smiling slavishly at Prissy, "could you give us the spelling of the word 'chrysanthemum'?"

Prissy rose nervously. Spelling was not her strong point.

"C - h - i . . . No! C - h - r - i - s . . . Oh gosh! . . . a - n - s - amum . . . ," she said all in a tizzy.

"Gilbert?" faltered poor Mr. Phillips, trying to conceal his disappointment. Gilbert stood up. "C-h-r-y-s-a-n-t-h-a-m-u-m" he said confidently.

Mr. Phillips' brow darkened. "Anne?" he enquired. Anne didn't hesitate.

"C-h-r-y-s-a-n-t-h-E-m-u-m!"

"Correct," said Mr. Phillips in amazement.

With a smug toss of her head, Anne sat down. Josie Pye looked crestfallen.

"Hey, Anne!" she jeered later, as Anne and Diana prepared to set off for home, "How d'you spell 'freckles?' "

"Hey Josie!" retorted Diana, quick as a flash, "How d'you spell 'ugly?' "

Gilbert ran after the two girls. "Congratulations on the spelling test, Anne," he said warmly.

Anne nodded at him with icy disdain. "Thank you, Mr. Blythe. But allow me to inform you that next time I shall be first in every subject." Grasping firm hold of Diana's arm, she marched off home. She had evidently made up her mind to hate Gilbert Blythe to the end of her life.

"Don't we have enough flowers right outside our door, Anne?" asked Marilla, as she came downstairs one bright Summer afternoon, dressed in her Sunday finery. Anne paused in her arrangement of a bouquet of wild blossoms.

"I want the house to look truly flowery to impress Diana," she explained. For Diana was expected to tea that very afternoon, and Anne, wearing her second best dress in honour of the occasion, was to be sole hostess. "May I use the rosebud-spray tea set, Marilla?" she asked.

"No indeed! The everyday set will do well enough for your company," answered Marilla, drawing on her gloves. "But you may have the fruit cake and the cherry preserves. And there's a bottle of raspberry cordial on the shelf in the kitchen."

"Oh Marilla," Anne clasped her hands, "how perfectly lovely! It will all seem so nice and grown-uppish."

Marilla adjusted her hat in the hall mirror. "Now don't forget to tell Matthew that Mrs. Allan will drive me back from the Ladies Aid. And remember to see that Matthew and Jerry Buote's supper is laid out for them."

A prim knock sounded on the front door. It was Diana, dressed in *her* second best dress and looking exactly as it is proper to look when asked out to tea.

"Have a lovely afternoon ladies," smiled Marilla, taking her leave.

The girls shook hands gravely, as if they had never met before. "Please come in and make yourself comfortable," said Anne in her best hostess manner.

"Why, thank you, how kind of you," answered Diana formally.

Once in the sitting room, both would-be ladies sat stiffly together, their hands folded just so in their laps, their toes in position. But polite enquiries as to Mrs. Barry's health and Matthew's potato crop failed to hold their attention for very long, and pretty soon they had abandoned their attempt at dignity and were talking and laughing as usual.

"It isn't good manners to tell your guests what you're serving, so I won't tell you what Marilla said we could have to drink. But it begins with a **r** and a **c** and it's a bright red colour," announced Anne, jumping up and running to look for the promised liquid.

It wasn't on the second shelf of the cupboard, where she expected it to be. Search revealed it away back on the top shelf. Anne placed the unlabelled bottle with a tumbler on a tray, and set it on a table near Diana.

"Oh, raspberry cordial, my favourite!" exclaimed Diana delightedly.

"I'm really glad you like it," said Anne politely. "I've never tasted it before in my life. I shall have to wait, though, because first I have to run out and stir the fire up. You take as much as you want, Diana."

When Anne came back from the kitchen with the tea tray, Diana was drinking her second glass of cordial. She made no

objection when Anne offered her a third. The tumblerfuls were generous ones and the red liquid delicious.

"The nicest I ever drank," announced Diana. Her words sounded a trifle slurred. "It's ever so much nicer than Mrs. Lynde's although she brags of hers so much. It doesn't taste a bit like hers."

"That's probably because Marilla is a much better cook," said Anne loyally, as she poured the tea. "Why Diana, whatever is the matter?" For Diana had stood up, swaying slightly. Then she sat down again very suddenly, holding onto her stomach.

"I'm awful sick," she announced thickly, "I . . . I gotta go home!" But instead of standing up again, she slumped over in a most unladylike manner.

"Oh, but you mustn't dream of going home without your tea," cried Anne in distress. "And here, you must try some fruit-cake and some of the cherry preserves!" She thrust a plateful of the sweet-smelling delicacies under Diana's nose. Diana's nostrils widened and she buried her face in her lace-trimmed handkerchief.

"Perhaps you need a little more cordial," suggested Anne helpfully. She poured another tumblerful and watched as Diana obediently drank it down. But instead of helping, the cordial seemed to make Diana feel worse. Before Anne's horrified eyes she keeled over sideways and landed flat on her face on the sofa.

"I must go home . . . . " she mumbled, her eyes closing.

"No, no, Diana. You stretch out on the sofa for a little while and you'll feel better. Where does it hurt?"

"The nicest I ever drank"

"She's drunk!"

Mrs. Rachel the town gossip, was also chairwoman of the temperance society.

Diana's answer was lost in the sofa cushions. Only the word 'home' was audible.

"I never heard of company going home without tea!" mourned Anne, "Oh Diana, please do stay!" But Diana heaved herself off the sofa, pushed past Anne and groped her way toward the hall door. She seemed to walk very strangely.

With tears of disappointment in her eyes, Anne fetched Diana's hat and parasol and hurried after her.

Mrs. Barry, Diana's mother, was enjoying her afternoon with Mrs. Lynde. Seated on the Barry porch, they had spent their time working on a quilt and dissecting the reputations of the people of Avonlea.

All of a sudden she heard Diana's returning footsteps. Glancing up she saw her daughter stagger up the porch steps and stand in front of her, swaying back and forth, like a . . . like a . . . .

"Drunk! Why she's drunk as a coot!" screamed Rachel Lynde, who had dropped her quilting and darted over to steady the swaying girl. In so doing, she had received a full blast of Diana's alcohol-laden breath.

"My Diana? No! It isn't possible . . . ." whispered Mrs. Barry, who felt as if she had just awakened into a nightmare. But there was Diana clapping her hand over her mouth and running back down the steps to be violently ill all over Mrs. Barry's prized azaleas. And there was that Anne Shirley, standing on the porch now, her big eyes fixed anxiously on Diana.

"Anne Shirley," hissed Mrs. Barry, "what did you give my Diana to drink?"

"Only raspberry cordial, Mrs. Barry," faltered Anne.

"Raspberry cordial my foot!" snorted Rachel Lynde. "Why that girl smells like Jake Griffith's distillery!"

With the startling clarity of a nightmare, it occurred to Mrs. Barry that not only was Mrs. Rachel the town gossip, she was also chairwoman of the temperance society. The good name of Barry was destroyed forever. And Mrs. Barry knew exactly who was to blame.

"You are a wicked, wicked girl, Anne Shirley," she flashed. "I should never have let Diana associate with an orphan like you. She will never do so again. Now leave this property at once!"

Words of protest sprang to Anne's lips. But the hostility and outrage she read on both adult faces silenced her. Very carefully, she placed Diana's hat and parasol on the front steps. Then she turned and fled.

When Marilla came home that evening, she found Anne lying on the sofa weeping as though her heart would break.

"Whatever has gone wrong now, Anne?" she queried in doubt and dismay. "I do hope you haven't been saucy to Mrs. Rachel again."

No answer from Anne save more tears and stormier sobs!

"Anne Shirley, when I ask you a question I want to be answered! Sit right up this very minute and tell me what you are crying about."

Anne sat up, tragedy personified.

"Mrs. Barry says that I set Diana drunk," she wailed. "And she says I must be a thoroughly bad, wicked girl, and she's never going to let Diana play with me again. Oh, Marilla, I'm just overcome with woe."

Marilla stared in blank amazement. "Drunk!" she said, when she had found her voice. "What on earth did you give her to drink?"

"Nothing but raspberry cordial," sobbed Anne. "I never thought it would make her drunk, Marilla, even if she did drink three big tumblerfuls."

Marilla marched into the kitchen and returned with the offending bottle. Her face was twitching in spite of herself.

"You certainly have a genius for trouble, child," she announced. "This is currant wine, not raspberry cordial. I probably put the cordial in the cellar myself instead of on the shelf in the cupboard. Now stop crying, Anne. It's not your fault. I'll go over and explain the mistake to Mrs. Barry."

But Mrs. Barry was not interested in Marilla's explanations.

"That Anne Shirley is a sly, deceitful child, and she's pulled the wool well over your eyes, Marilla," she snapped.

Rachel Lynde was determined to put her oar in too.

"I've warned you before about that currant wine, Marilla," she announced self-righteously. "It's the demon liquor that's at fault here, and if you didn't insist on making that wine . . . " This was more than Marilla could take.

"My currant wine is famous all over this island, as well you know, Rachel Lynde!" she broke in. "Why even the Reverend Allan himself takes a drop when he comes calling. And as to Christian virtue, making a little wine for refreshment is far less sinful than meddling in other people's affairs!" There was a moment's stunned silence. Before either woman could gather her wits for a suitably stinging reply, Marilla turned on her heel and swept from the Barry home in a storm of indignation.

The next afternoon, Anne, busy with her household chores, happened to glance out the kitchen window. She was astonished to see Diana waving frantically from the nearby field. In a trice, Anne was out of the house and running to meet her friend, hope springing up in her heart. The hope faded when she saw Diana's dejected expression.

"Your mother hasn't forgiven me, then?" she asked.

Diana shook her head. "No, Anne. I told her it wasn't your fault and I cried and cried. But it's no use. We can't ever be friends again."

"Oh Diana," said Anne tearfully. "We must stay secret friends at least. Will you swear to be my secret bosom friend?"

Diana looked even more troubled. "But isn't it wicked to swear?" she asked doubtfully. "We're in enough trouble already."

"Not if you're swearing a vow," Anne assured her. Taking Diana's hand in her own, she intoned: "I solemnly swear to remain faithful to my bosom friend Diana Barry as long as the sun and the moon shall endure. Now you say it, Diana."

When Diana had repeated the vow to Anne's satisfaction, Anne pulled out her little patchwork scissors from her apron pocket. "Now wilt thou give me a lock of thy jet black tresses?"

"Fare thee well, my beloved friend. My heart will be ever faithful to thee."

she enquired soulfully.

"But I don't have any black dresses," objected Diana, puzzled.

"Your hair, silly," said Anne, temporarily dropping her tragic-actress voice.

"Oh. My hair. Yes, of course," agreed Diana.

After the hair-cutting ceremony was over, the friends hugged each other sadly. Then Anne stood and watched Diana run out of sight. Their romantic parting had been almost as satisfying as if Mrs. Barry had wept and forgiven her. "Fare thee well, my beloved friend," she whispered. "Henceforth we must be as strangers, living side by side. But my heart will be ever faithful to thee."

Anne had expected to die from grief at being parted from her bosom friend. Much to her own surprise, she survived. But as week followed lonely week and Mrs. Barry still did not relent, Anne found she missed Diana more and more. Partly to distract herself from her sense of loss, and partly out of a natural desire to learn, she flung herself heart and soul into her studies.

With the new school year came a new teacher, and in Miss Stacey, Anne found a bright and helpful guide. "I want to look back on this class as having been the most imaginative, the most committed students on Prince Edward Island," Miss Stacey had said that first morning, as she introduced herself, and Anne's soul had expanded like a flower.

"She has such a gentle voice, and when she says my name, I feel instinctively that she's spelling it with an **e**," Anne had confided to Matthew.

Miss Stacey was aware that there was some trouble between Diana and Anne. But it wasn't until she had a visit from Mrs. Barry, warning her to forbid all association between the two girls, that she began to understand where the trouble lay. She mentioned Mrs. Barry's visit to Anne one day after school. "I don't think, Anne" she said with a smile, "that Mrs. Barry entirely approves of you."

She had found in her new teacher another kindred spirit.

Anne sighed. "I'm afraid you're right, Miss Stacey," she agreed, "but then I don't think God Himself would meet entirely with Mrs. Barry's approval." She was silent for a moment. "I think I can cope with the social persecution of being an orphan," she added slowly, "I've grown used to that. But it's a terrible injustice to be falsely accused."

"What we must bear in mind, Anne," said Miss Stacey, "is that all these trials and troubles that pop up in our lives often serve a useful purpose. They build character. And remember, tomorrow is always fresh with no mistakes in it."

"It's just that I miss Diana terribly, Miss Stacey."

Miss Stacey patted Anne's hand. "Don't lose heart, child. Diana will always be your friend, no matter what anyone accuses you of. In the end, the truth will set you free."

"The truth will set you free," echoed Anne, touched by the beauty of the words as much as by Miss Stacey's compassion. She felt warmed by the knowledge that she had found in her new teacher another kindred spirit.

A few weeks after her talk with Miss Stacey, Anne was in the kitchen helping Marilla prepare dinner.

"Go fetch that left-over sauce from the pantry, child," instructed Marilla. "I'll warm it up for tonight's pudding."

Anne stepped into the pantry. As she picked up the bowl, she almost screamed in horror. For there, floating in the yellowy liquid, lay a drowned mouse. With a pang of guilt, Anne remembered that Marilla had asked her to cover the bowl the night before, when she was putting it away. Quickly she reached for a ladle, scooped out the pathetic corpse and wrapped it in newspaper, keeping her eyes averted all the time. Then she sneaked out of the house and buried the body in the yard.

Anne fully intended to confess her sin to Marilla, but just how to phrase it posed a problem. She reflected on this as she washed her hands at the sink.

"We've already tried sauce on *our* pudding, Marilla," she ventured brightly, "Perhaps it's only fair the pigs should be allowed some on *their* feed tonight."

Marilla stared at her. "Waste our precious pudding sauce on the pigs! Anne Shirley, have you taken leave of your senses?"

"I forgot to put the cheese cloth over it last night, Marilla. I was imagining I was a nun on my way to the altar to take the veil and . . . "

Marilla was no longer listening. Her attention had been distracted by a knock on the front door.

"Goodness gracious, I wonder who that could be at this hour," she said, taking off her apron and hurrying to answer.

The unexpected caller turned out to be Miss Stacey. In the excitement of seeing her beloved teacher step into the parlour at Green Gables, all thoughts of drowned mice and tainted sauce vanished from Anne's mind.

"I was just over at the Barrys', Miss Cuthbert," explained Miss Stacey, "and I thought I'd take this opportunity to stop by."

Marilla's heart sank. "What's she been up to now, Miss Stacey? Don't tell me this misunderstanding with the Barry family has made her neglect her studies."

Miss Stacey smiled. "Quite the contrary, Miss Cuthbert. Anne's work is excellent, which is why I'm here. I wondered whether you would permit her to join a special class? You see, I intend to give extra tutoring after school to those students who wish to take the entrance exams for Queen's."

The wariness in Marilla's eyes gave way to surprise. "The College in Charlottetown? Our Anne?"

"Your Anne is bright and energetic and very determined," replied Miss Stacey, "I think she could pass as a teacher or even go on to the University."

Marilla's smile was dazzling. "Why, of course," she beamed, "of course she can join the class if she wants to." Then Marilla, radiating pride, had insisted Miss Stacey join them for supper. Supper had passed in a flurry of chatter and gaiety. Even tongue-tied Matthew had joined in the conversation once or twice.

It wasn't until Marilla was actually carrying in the dessert: the pudding in one hand and the pitcher of *warmed-up* sauce in

"Don't eat it, Miss Stacey!"

the other, that Anne, fear striking at her heart, suddenly remembered the miserable mouse. Dumb with horror, she saw Marilla pour sauce over Miss Stacey's portion of pudding. Hypnotized, she watched as Miss Stacey raised the spoon to her lips. Then just as Miss Stacey opened her mouth, Anne found her voice:

"DON'T EAT IT, MISS STACEY!" she screamed at the top of her lungs.

Miss Stacey's spoon clattered to her plate. Marilla pushed back her chair. "Anne Shirley, what is wrong with you," she demanded, turning red as fire.

"A mouse drowned in the sauce, Marilla," moaned Anne, "I was working up courage to tell you, when Miss Stacey came in and told us all about studying for Queen's and then I . . . Why Miss Stacey . . ., " she paused, her attention completely distracted, "Whatever is the matter?"

For Miss Stacey had buried her face in her table napkin. Her shoulders were shaking. Anne turned to Matthew for guidance. Tears were trickling down his cheeks. In utter bewilderment she appealed to Marilla. But Marilla's eyes were closed. Her head was thrown back and her whole body was convulsed with laughter. Anne stared at them all, baffled. Then she shrugged. "I suppose in the end it was a romantic way to perish," she concluded doubtfully, "for a mouse."

As winter set in, the small group of would-be Queen's scholars set to work with a will under Miss Stacey's expert guidance. Anne truly enjoyed studying. When the regular day students had gone home, she liked nothing better than to move with the five or six remaining pupils to the front of the class. She loved the quiet scratching of Miss Stacey's chalk on the board, the silent concentration of the others around her, and the warm glow of the schoolroom as the light darkened outside. The only flaw in her happiness was that Mrs. Barry had refused to let Diana study for the entrance to Queen's.

"Mother says I should concentrate on learning to run a

household instead of always having my nose stuck in a book." Diana had confided in a brief conversation, snatched while the day students were preparing to go home.

"Oh Diana," grieved Anne, "I feel as though you've tasted the bitterness of death."

As she watched Diana go slowly out with the others, to walk alone along the paths they had so often trod together, Anne felt a lump come into her throat. Hastily she retired behind the pages of her Latin grammar. Not for worlds would Anne have had Gilbert Blythe or Josie Pye or any of the other aspiring Queen's scholars see the tears that filled her eyes.

That winter, a mass meeting was organised in Charlottetown in honour of the Prime Minister's visit to Prince Edward Island. In the firm belief that no gathering of any kind could succeed without her, Mrs. Rachel Lynde insisted on going. She took her husband, Thomas, with her. Thomas would be useful in looking after the horse. Marilla, who had a genuine interest in politics, went along too. She left Anne and Matthew to keep house alone until her return the following day.

"What way do *you* vote, Matthew?" asked Anne that evening.

A bright fire was glowing in the grate, and blue-white frost crystals were shining on the windowpanes. Matthew was nodding over a copy of the *Farmers' Advocate*, while Anne was supposed to be studying her geometry.

"Conservative," said Matthew, blinking awake.

"Then I'm Conservative, too," said Anne decidedly. "I'm glad because Gil — I mean some of the boys at school are Grits. Ruby Gillis says that when a man is courting he always has to agree with the girl's mother in religion and her father in politics. Ruby Gillis knows all about courting because she has three older sisters. Did you ever go courting, Matthew?"

"Well now, no, I dunno's I ever did," said Matthew, who had certainly never thought of such a thing in his whole existence.

"Never ever? Why not, Matthew?"

"Well now, I couldn't do it without *talking* to a girl."

"What a great loss," Anne shook her head sadly. "I'm sure there were many broken hearts on this Island as a result."

Matthew blushed and concentrated fiercely on his *Farmers' Advocate*. For a while Anne gazed into the fire, then returned her attention reluctantly to her geometry.

A few moments later, the harmonious silence was interrupted by the sound of flying footsteps on the icy boardwalk outside. The next instant the kitchen door was flung open and in rushed Diana Barry, white-faced and breathless, a shawl wrapped hastily around her head.

"Oh Anne, do come quick," she implored. My little sister is awful sick. She's got croup, Mary Joe says. Father and mother are away at the rally and there's nobody to go for the doctor."

Without a word, Matthew reached out for cap and coat, slipped past Diana and away into the darkness of the yard.

"He's gone to harness the mare to go to Carmody for the doctor," said Anne, who was pulling on her warm, hooded jacket. "We're such kindred spirits I can read his thoughts."

"I don't believe he'll find the doctor at Carmody," sobbed Diana. "He's probably at the rally too! Oh Anne, I'm so scared. Poor little Minnie May can't breathe!"

Anne was unlocking the medicine chest. "Don't forget that Mrs. Hammond had three sets of twins. When you look after all those babies you naturally get a lot of experience. Now just calm down, Diana. I know the Ipecac is here somewhere. It's an expectorant you see," she added knowledgeably, producing the bottle from the back of the cabinet. "It helps you cough up whatever's blocking your breathing." She stuffed the bottle of medicine into her coat pocket, then grasped Diana's hand. Together they hastened out into the darkness.

The night was clear and frosty, all ebony of shadow and silver of snowy slope. Big stars were shining over the silent fields. Here and there black pointed firs stood up with snow powdering their branches and the wind whistling through them. Although truly worried about Diana's sister, Anne could not help responding to the night's mystery and loveliness and to the sweetness of sharing it all with her closest friend, who had been so long a stranger.

Minnie May was really very sick. Her hoarse breathing could be heard all over the house. Anne went to work with skill and promptness.

"Mary Joe, you may put some wood on the fire," she instructed the bewildered mother's helper. "I don't want to hurt your feelings, but it seems to me you should have thought of it before, if you'd any imagination. You try to find some soft flannel cloths, Diana. I'm going to give Minnie May a good dose of Ipecac."

Minnie May did not take kindly to the Ipecac, but Anne had not brought up three sets of twins for nothing. Down that Ipecac went, not only once, but many times during the long, anxious night.

It was three o'clock before Matthew arrived with the doctor. He had been obliged to go all the way to Spencervale for one. By this time, the pressing need for help had passed. Minnie May was much better and was sleeping soundly.

"I was awfully near giving up in despair," explained Anne to the doctor, as he listened to Minnie May's chest. "She got worse and worse until she was sicker than ever the Hammond twins were. I actually thought she was going to choke to death. I gave her every drop of Ipecac in that bottle. When the last dose went down, I had almost given up hope. But in about three minutes she coughed up the phlegm and began to get better right away. You must just imagine my relief, doctor. Some things cannot be expressed in words."

"Yes, I know," nodded the doctor. He looked at Anne as if he were thinking some things about her that couldn't be expressed either. Later on, though, when Mrs. Barry returned, he managed to find just the right words. "I tell you, that little red-headed girl saved your baby's life. It would have been too late by the time I got there," he said.

Mrs. Barry had stroked Minnie May's head tenderly and swallowed hard.

In the white-frosted winter dawn, Anne drove home with Matthew.

"Isn't it a wonderful morning, Matthew?" she sighed, as the sleigh sped across the snow-covered fields, "Doesn't the whole world look like something God had just imagined for His own pleasure? I'm really sorry I was ever cross with Mrs. Hammond for having twins. If she hadn't, I mightn't have known what to do for Minnie May. But oh, Matthew, I'm so sleepy, I can't go to school. I just know I couldn't keep my eyes open. But I hate to stay home . . . Gil—some of the others—will get ahead of me and . . . ."

Anne fell asleep in mid-sentence. Matthew gazed down fondly at the small white face with the dark shadows under the eyes. Very gently he put one arm around her to prevent her falling out of the sleigh.

It was well on in the white and rosy winter afternoon when Anne awoke and came down to the kitchen. Marilla looked up from her knitting. Her eyes were merry. "Mrs. Barry's been over here, begging to see you. But I wasn't about to wake you. You're invited over for dinner, Anne." She chuckled, "I imagine humble pie is on the menu."

Anne rushed to the door. "Oh Marilla! Can I go right now? Before I do my chores? I'm simply aching to see Diana!"

"Run along, child," said Marilla indulgently. But Anne was already out the door and tearing through the orchard, her hair streaming behind her.

Marilla was right. Humble pie was indeed on the menu at the Barry household. Mrs. Barry kissed Anne and cried and apologized for ever doubting her word.

"I felt fearfully embarrassed, Marilla," Anne recounted later, when she got home that night, "but I just assured her that I had never meant to intoxicate Diana, and that I was ready to cover the past with a mantle of oblivion. And Mrs. Barry put the very best china out. Just as if I was real company. I can't tell you what a thrill it gave me. Nobody ever used their very best china on my account before."

But the biggest thrill of all had come when Mrs. Barry had invited Anne to accompany them to the Christmas Ball at Carmody.

"She said they'd be honoured if I would stay overnight with Diana, too," Anne finished. "It's going to be a very special occasion, and I'm to be their guest of honour."

Marilla's response was unexpectedly harsh. "You can calm down because you're not going," she declared flatly, her eyes fixed on her knitting. "For a woman so firmly against currant wine, she's being strangely indulgent, I must say. I'm surprised she's allowing Diana to go. A ball is for adults, not children."

"But Marilla," pleaded Anne, "It's Christmas! And I'm to be the guest of honour. I'm invited to spend the night! In the spare room bed too! Think of the honour of your Anne being put in the spare-room bed!"

"Well, it's just an honour you'll have to forgo," said Marilla firmly. "You heard what I said, Anne. Now off to bed."

Anne looked at Matthew imploringly. But Matthew's attention seemed miles away. He was chewing thoughtfully on his pipe-stem, staring into the fire.

"This is a wound I shall bear forever," sighed Anne tragically, as she trudged off to bed.

When the door had closed behind her, Matthew removed his pipe from his mouth. "Well now, Marilla," he said. "I think you ought to let her go."

"Who's bringing this child up, you or me?" retorted Marilla. "That Mrs. Barry just wants to ease her conscience and I'm not going to allow it."

Matthew clamped his lips round his pipe and drew on it in silence.

"And no amount of huffing and puffing from you is going to change my mind," snapped Marilla, "You'd let her go to the moon if she had the notion. Well, I don't approve of balls. She'd just have her head filled up with nonsense."

Matthew cleared his throat. "Fact is, Marilla," he said slowly, "you never went to a ball. Fact is this whole idea's got you scared to death."

'I think you ought to let her go."

"You'd let her go to the moon if she had the notion. Well, I don't approve of balls."

Marilla put down her knitting and stared at her brother in shock.

"That little girl oughta have all the kindness we can give her," continued Matthew. "We got no call to raise her as cheerless as we was. Besides it's Christmas. I think you ought to let her go."

For once, no quick reply sprang to Marilla's lips.

Anne was washing dishes in martyred silence the next morning, when Marilla entered the kitchen. "Very well," she said curtly to Anne's reproachful back. "You may go."

Anne whirled around, dripping dishcloth in hand, "Oh Marilla, say those blessed words again!" she exclaimed.

"I guess once is enough to say them," replied Marilla. "This is Matthew's doing and I wash my hands of it. If you catch pneumonia sleeping in a strange bed or coming out of that overheated hall in the middle of the night, don't blame me. Blame Matthew."

"I dreamt last night that I arrived at the ball in puffed sleeves."

"I dreamt last night that I arrived at the ball in puffed sleeves," confided Anne, "and everyone was overcome by my regal entrance."

"Regal my eye!" sniffed Marilla. "You're dripping greasy dishwater all over my nice clean floor, Anne Shirley. And if I have to listen to any more of this puffed-sleeve nonsense, I'll just change my mind, that's what I'll do!"

Anne returned meekly to her dishes, determined never to mention the longed-for sleeves again.

Matthew was covered in confusion. He had deliberately chosen Samuel Lawson's store, feeling sure that either Samuel or his son would wait on him. Alas! the door had closed behind him and instead of being greeted by a solid, comfortable man, Matthew could see a lady clerk stalking him from behind the counter. A very dashing young person she was too, with big, rolling brown eyes and a most generous and bewildering smile. She was dressed with exceeding smartness and wore several bangle bracelets that glittered and tinkled and completely wrecked Matthew's wits.

"What can I do for you, Mr. Cuthbert?" enquired this person, whose name was Lucilla Harris. She tapped the counter briskly with both hands. The bracelets rattled and clattered.

"Well now . . . I'd . . . Uh . . . like . . . Uh . . . have you got any garden rakes?" stammered Matthew.

"We don't usually carry rakes in December," responded Miss Harris, "but I'll go check upstairs. We may have one or two in storage."

During her absence, Matthew collected his senses for another try.

"Anything else, Mr. Cuthbert?" enquired Lucilla, when she returned bearing the last rake in the store.

"Well now, since you suggest it, I . . . uh . . . that is . . . I . . . " Matthew dropped his voice, "I may as well take some hayseed."

Miss Harris had heard Matthew Cuthbert called odd. She now decided he was entirely crazy. "We only keep hayseed in the spring," she explained loftily, "We've none on hand just now."

Matthew rallied his powers for a final attempt. "Well now, if it isn't too much trouble I'd . . . uh . . . uh . . . I'd like to look at . . . uh . . . look at . . . some sugar, yes, some sugar."

"White or brown?" asked Miss Harris patiently.

Beads of perspiration stood out on Matthew's forehead.

"Which would you suggest?" he enquired desperately.

"There's a barrel of brown over there," said Miss Harris, shaking her bangles at it. "It's the only kind we have in stock."

"I'll . . . I'll take 20 pounds of it. Yes, 20 pounds," decided Matthew fervently. As Miss Harris was totting up his bill, Matthew cast a final frantic look around the store. Then he leaned over the counter toward Miss Harris' ear. "I need a dress!" he gasped. Miss Harris gazed at him in shock. "With puffed sleeves!" croaked Matthew. "For Anne," he added quickly, seeing her expression. Miss Harris passed a hand over her eyes. Her bangles tinkled delicately.

"Land sakes, Mr. Cuthbert," she smiled, "why didn't you say so in the first place. Now you come over here with me to the window. I've got just the thing. Puffed sleeves, did you say?"

"You are a man of impeccable taste, Matthew."

Anne stared at the dress in disbelief. How pretty it was—a lovely cloudy blue with all the gloss of silk; a skirt with dainty frills and shirrings; a waist elaborately pin-tucked in the most fashionable way, with a ruffle of filmy lace at the neck. But the sleeves were the crowning glory! They had long elbow cuffs, and above them two beautiful puffs, divided by bows of blue silk ribbon. Could it really be for her?

Quickly she slipped it on and ran downstairs. Marilla stood at the kitchen table contemplating a giant bag of brown sugar.

"Marilla, just look at these puffs!" Anne twirled in delight around the kitchen.

Marilla snorted. "They're ridiculous. As big as balloons! You'll have to turn sideways to get through the doors!"

All the same, she couldn't help noticing how graceful Anne looked in the longer skirt. "She's growing up real straight and slim," she thought with pride as Anne hurried off to thank Matthew.

Anne found Matthew in the barn. From a window high up in the eaves, a shaft of wintry sunlight pierced the quiet dimness, setting the dust-motes dancing and falling on Matthew's stooped figure, as he bent over a sack of grain. Anne felt as though her dress lit the whole barn with a blaze of blue.

Matthew looked up as she came in and grinned with pleasure. "Well now, I guess I shoulda waited till Christmas, but I thought you might want to wear it to the ball. Why . . . why . . . don't you like it?" he asked, suddenly concerned. For Anne's eyes had filled with tears.

"Like it? Oh, Matthew!" Anne clasped her hands. "It's more exquisite than any dress I could ever imagine."

In that instant Matthew felt that all his suffering in the Lawson store had been worthwhile. He nodded his head toward Anne's elbows.

"Puffed sleeves," he noted, in the tone of an expert.

"The puffiest in the world," exulted Anne. "You are a man of impeccable taste, Matthew."

Very shyly, Matthew bent down and kissed the top of Anne's head. "Mustn't get your dress dirty," he said gruffly. But Anne, forgetting all about her new dress in the rush of love she felt for him, threw her arms about Matthew and hugged him tightly.

The night of the ball passed like a beautiful dream for Anne. Clutching their dance cards, their eyes ashine, and their hair gleaming, she and Diana had watched in dazed admiration as the dancers swirled around the floor.

Anne was delightfully conscious that no-one in the room had puffier sleeves than she did. Diana felt a twinge of jealousy at the sight of Alice Bell's new hair style.

"I think she looks ridiculous," she declared to Anne. "She's only seventeen and she's put her hair up already. I'm going to wait till I'm eighteen."

But Anne's attention was elsewhere. She had caught sight

Anne assured Diana she certainly didn't care to dance with Gilbert Blythe.

of Gilbert Blythe dancing with Josie Pye. She pretended not to notice, but somehow she felt as if her puffed sleeves had lost some of their puff.

"It's too bad you've been so awful to him," said Diana, whose sharp eyes had noticed the direction of Anne's glance; "he might have asked you to dance."

Anne only tossed her head and assured Diana she certainly didn't care to dance with Gilbert Blythe. This turned out to be just as well, for Gilbert studiously ignored Anne all night. Perhaps he felt it was time to give her a taste of her own medicine. Anne and Diana danced with each other instead, and what with trying to keep time to the lilting music and not step on each other's toes, the evening passed in a whirl of laughter.

Perhaps because he did his best to *appear* to have a good time, Gilbert found the ball rather a strain. As he stood at the edge of the room, trying to decide whom he ought to dance with next, he caught sight of Anne's dance card, lying abandoned on the refreshments table. Picking it up, he folded it in two, then placed it carefully in his breast pocket.

It was very late when the girls returned to Diana's house. Mr. and Mrs. Barry went instantly to bed. But the small parlour, which opened into the spare room, was pleasantly warm and dimly lighted by the embers of a fire in the grate. Anne and Diana tiptoed in and changed into their night clothes by its glow.

"I bet Gilbert took your dance card and that's why you couldn't find it!" Diana giggled, as she waltzed lightly around the shadowy room.

"Such a romantic gesture would be beyond his imagination," sniffed Anne. But that hope had occurred to her, too.

"Well who then? Josie Pye?" persisted Diana giddily.

Anne had no intention of discussing the matter further. "How about I race you to bed? I'll just bet I get to jump in first!" she suggested brightly. "On your marks, get set, GO!"

Two white-clad figures flew down the long room, through the spare room door, and bounded on the bed at the same moment. And then—something moved beneath them. There was a gasp and a cry, and a voice was saying in muffled tones: "Merciful goodness!"

Anne and Diana were never able to tell how they got off that bed and out of the room. They only knew that after one frantic rush, they found themselves creeping upstairs.

"Oh, who was it? *What* was it?" whispered Anne, her teeth chattering with cold and fright.

"It was Aunt Josephine," said Diana, gasping with laughter. "We weren't expecting her till tomorrow. I know she's going to be absolutely furious about this, and . . . oh dear!" Diana's giggles stopped abruptly. "I suppose I shall have to wave goodbye to my music lessons now."

"What music lessons?" shivered Anne.

"I've always wanted music lessons, and Aunt Josephine promised I should have some. She's the only one in our family who's rich enough to pay for them, you see."

"It was my fault, Diana. I won't have you lose your music lessons because of me." It seemed to Anne that Diana had been deprived of enough lessons already. "I'll just have to have a talk with your Aunt Josephine in the morning."

"Anne Shirley, you'd never! Why, she'll eat you alive!" protested Diana. "She's awfully prim and proper. Now hush!" she whispered, putting her finger to her lips and opening the door to the room she shared with her sister. "You're just going to have to sleep with Minnie May tonight. And don't move a muscle—because she kicks like a mule."

Anne felt like she was walking in to a dragon's den when she approached Aunt Josephine's room the next morning. But she screwed up her courage and knocked. A sharp "Come in" followed. Miss Josephine Barry, thin, prim, and rigid, wheeled round from the desk where she had been writing.

Her eyes snapped as she surveyed her visitor from top to toe. "What's this?" she growled. "Come to finish the job have you?"

Whatever little courage Anne had mustered, drained away.

"I am not interested in the confessions of assassins who masquerade as little girls."

"I'm sorry I startled you, ma'am," she whispered.

"Who are you?" demanded the dragon.

"Anne of Green Gables," Anne twisted her fingers together nervously, "and I've come to confess."

"I am not interested," pronounced the dragon, "in the confessions of assassins who masquerade as little girls."

"It was all my fault about jumping into bed on you, Miss Barry. I suggested it. Diana would never have thought of such a thing. Diana is far too lady-like. So I think you ought to forgive her and let her have her music lessons back. Diana's heart is set on music lessons, and I know too well what it is to set your heart on a thing and not get it. If you must be cross with someone, be cross with me. I've been so used in my early days to having people cross at me that I can endure it much better than Diana can."

Much of the snap had gone out of the old lady's eyes by this time. It was replaced by a hint of amusement. But her tone was still severe.

"Do you know what it is to be awakened out of a sound sleep, after a long and tiring journey, by two great girls coming bounce down on top of you?"

"I don't know, but I can imagine," said Anne eagerly. "I'm sure it must have been terrifying in the extreme. But then there *is* our side of it too." She stopped suddenly. "Have you any imagination, Miss Barry?"

"Imagination at my age is a threat to life," the old lady said drily.

"Well, if you *did* have imagination," continued Anne, "you'd be able to put yourself in our place. We didn't know there was anyone in that bed and you nearly scared us to death. And then we couldn't sleep in the spare room after being promised. I suppose you're used to sleeping in spare rooms. But just imagine what you would feel like if you were an orphan girl who'd never had such an honour. Mine was the sleep of the bitterly disappointed, Miss Barry. And to make matters worse, I was forced to lie awake all night with the knowledge that I had cost Diana her career as a world famous concert pianist."

All the snap had gone from the dragon by this time. Miss Barry actually laughed.

"I dare say your claim to sympathy is just as valid as mine, child. It all depends on the way we look at it."

"Then you'll forgive Diana?"

Miss Barry considered. "Very well; I will re-instate Diana's music lessons in exchange for you . . . " she patted Anne's hand, "coming up to Charlottetown to visit me on occasion."

"Me, Miss Barry?"

"Yes, you, Anne of Green Gables. Diana can come along as well. You amuse me, child. And precious little amuses me at my age. Will you come?"

Anne nodded her head eagerly.

"Then go tell Diana she can be a concert pianist after all."

Anne found Diana lurking in the hallway, where she had been listening to every word.

"You wouldn't think so to look at her," she whispered delightedly, "but your Aunt Josephine is definitely a kindred spirit! Isn't it splendid, Diana, kindred spirits aren't nearly so scarce as I used to believe!"

The winter months fled by, and soon spring had come once more to Green Gables, lingering along through April and May in a succession of sweet, fresh, chilly days with pink sunsets and miracles of recovery and growth.

Anne was growing, too, shooting up so rapidly that Marilla was constantly adjusting the hems of her skirts. "Why Anne, how you do grow!" she exclaimed one day in early June, as she was measuring Anne for a new dress of the palest green. A sigh followed on the words. Marilla felt a queer regret over Anne's inches. The child she had learned to love had vanished somehow and here was this slim, serious-eyed girl of fifteen in her place. Marilla was as attached to the girl as she had been attached to the child, but she was conscious of a sense of loss.

"You've only a few more days before the Entrance Examinations for Queen's," she said now. "Do you think you'll be able to get through?"

Anne shivered. "I don't know. Sometimes I think I'll be all right and sometimes I get horribly afraid. I wish it was all over, Marilla. It haunts me. Sometimes I wake up in the night and wonder what I'll do if I don't pass."

"Why, go to school next year and try again," said Marilla unconcernedly.

"I wouldn't have the heart for it. It would be such a disgrace to fail, especially if Gil—if the others passed."

A few days after her conversation with Marilla, Anne sat in the examination hall in Charlottetown, waiting for the question papers to be handed out. Once again the familiar cold fluttery feeling, which had kept her awake at night, swept over her. So much depended on the results of these exams. She dearly wanted to be admitted to Queen's so she could study to become a teacher. For the sake of Matthew and Marilla, she wanted to do well. But she also knew that success would be incomplete and bitter if she did not come out ahead of Gilbert Blythe. Watching Gilbert's profile as he bent over his desk, Anne realized that the old anger she had cherished against him for so long had vanished. Somewhere along the way her feelings toward him had changed. All that remained of the old resentment was a deep-rooted sense of competition.

It was this feeling of rivalry that caused Anne to strain every nerve during the week of examinations. So did Gilbert. They met and passed each other on the streets of Charlottetown a dozen times without any sign of recognition. Each time Anne held her head a little higher and wished a little more earnestly that she had made friends with Gilbert. And each time she vowed a little more determinedly to surpass him in the results.

Then suddenly the last exam was over. Students were thronging out of the gloomy examination hall into the June sunlight. Anne stood on the entrance steps, her relief mingled with regret. For beside her stood Miss Stacey, who would not be returning to Avonlea school in the fall. "I'm going to miss you tremendously, Miss Stacey," she said, "I feel you've given me so much."

Miss Stacey smiled her warm quick smile. "I want to wish you all the luck in the world, Anne Shirley. If anyone deserves to be successful, it's you. I'll be watching out for you, even from Halifax."

"Do you really have to go? It seems so far," protested Anne.

Miss Stacey's brown eyes clouded for the merest fraction of a second. "I have my own set of troubles," she admitted, "My mother is very ill, very ill indeed. But remember, Anne . . . ," the smile was back, "true friends are always together in spirit."

"But remember, Anne, true friends are always together in spirit."

Below them, on the sun-speckled lawn, Gilbert waited to say his goodbyes to Miss Stacey. For him, too, she had proved a wise and kindly guide.

Looking down at him now, she glanced back at Anne. "I want to remind you of something we once agreed upon together, Anne Shirley," she said. "Tomorrow is always fresh with no mistakes in it." Taking Anne in her arms, she hugged her affectionately. Then she was gone, striding down the steps toward Gilbert.

Staring after her, Anne couldn't help thinking how much less lonely it might have been if she and Gilbert could have said goodbye to Miss Stacey together.

The examination results would not be known for at least two weeks, when the pass list would be published in the newspaper, for all the world to see. At first Anne felt that the suspense would be more than she could bear. But as the summer days wore on, examinations and high marks lost some of their importance in the delight of rowing and berrying and dreaming to her heart's content.

She and Diana fairly lived outdoors, spending most of their time on or about the pond. It was splendid to fish for trout over the bridge and the two girls learned to row themselves about in the little flat-bottomed dory belonging to Mr. Barry.

Ruby Gillis and Jane Andrews came over to visit one sunny

*In her right hand the lily,
in her left
The letter — all her bright
hair streaming down.*

afternoon, and Anne, inspired by the increase in potential players, suggested they dramatize the sad story of Elaine, the Lily Maid. Ever since she could read, Anne had loved Tennyson's poetry, especially everything he had written about the legend of King Arthur. She was devoured by secret regret that she had not been born in Camelot. Those ancient days of Merlin and Arthur, Guinevere and Lancelot seemed so much more romantic than the present.

The other girls were all familiar with *Lancelot and Elaine*, too, as they had studied the poem in school the previous winter. Anne's plan was hailed with enthusiasm. They gathered together all the necessary props, then stood by the flat-bottomed dory, arguing over who should play the tragic heroine.

"Ruby, you must be Elaine, because you're so fair," Anne commanded.

"I couldn't lie there and pretend I was dead," protested Ruby, "I'd die of fright!"

"You should be Elaine, Anne," declared Diana, "your complexion's just as fair as Ruby's and your hair's much darker than plain old red now."

"Really? Do you really think so?" asked Anne, flushing with delight.

"It's definitely auburn," agreed Jane loyally, "and that's pretty close to blonde."

"Very well, then." Anne stepped regally into the boat, which had been draped in Mrs. Barry's old black shawl. (It was the nearest they could come to the 'blackest samite' or royal silk, mentioned in the poem.) She lay down, spreading her hair around her shoulders and closing her eyes.

"She does look really dead, doesn't she?" whispered Ruby Gillis nervously. She stared at the still, white face under the flickering shadows of the birches. "It makes me feel frightened. Do you suppose it's really right to act like this? Mrs. Lynde says that all play-acting is a sin."

"You're spoiling the effect, Ruby," said the corpse severely. "This is hundreds of years before Mrs. Lynde was born. Diana, you arrange the rest. It's ridiculous for Elaine to be talking when she's dead."

Diana rose to the occasion. Under her capable supervision, the old yellow piano scarf was draped carefully around the body. It wasn't exactly cloth of gold, as the poem demanded. But it made an excellent substitute. In Elaine's left hand they placed her letter to Lancelot; in her right, a bouquet of summer flowers. By rights, Elaine should have carried a single lily. But perfect white lilies did not grow in abundance near Orchard Slope. One by one the girls solemnly kissed the quiet brow. "Farewell for ever, sweet sister," they murmured in heart-broken tones. Then they pushed the barge off from the landing place. They waited only long enough to see it caught in the current, before scampering up through the woods, across the road and down to the lower headland, where they had arranged to await the lily maid.

As her barge drifted slowly downstream, Anne savoured the romance of the situation to the full. The summer sun stroked her face. The birds sang sweetly. Lines from the poem floated through her mind and she chanted them softly, like a song:

> In her right hand the lily, in her left
> The letter—all her bright hair streaming down.
> And all the coverlid was cloth of gold . . .
> She did not seem as dead
> But fast asleep, and lay as tho' she smiled . . . .

Somewhere, beyond the mists of romance, another song was sounding faintly. It was not a romantic song. It gurgled and muttered and coughed and reminded Anne unpleasantly of damp shoes and beds. With a start, she sat bolt upright. In the bottom of the barge yawned a huge hole, through which water was pouring noisily. It slurped and slapped all over Elaine's shoes and skirt, all over the blackest samite, all over the cloth of gold. At this rate the boat would sink long before it reached the lower headland. Anne cast around frantically for the oars. But they had been left behind at the landing. The current was moving swiftly now. Scanning the horizon desperately, Anne saw that the dory

was fast approaching the bridge. "Dear God," she prayed, "please take the boat close to a pile and I'll do the rest." The piles, which supported the bridge, were fashioned from tall old tree trunks, covered with branch stubs. If she could just get close enough to one of them, perhaps she could clamber on to it. A few more moments of terrifying rocking and pulling passed like months, and then . . . her prayer was answered. The boat banged into a pile. With one bound, Anne leaped from the dory and wrapped her arms tightly around the scratchy trunk. And there she hung for dear life.

The dory, relieved of the weight of its passenger, drifted on under the bridge, then sank gratefully in midstream. Ruby, Jane, and Diana, waiting for it on the lower headland, saw it disappear before their very eyes and had no doubt that Anne had gone down with it. For a moment they stood still, white as sheets, frozen with horror. Then, shrieking for help at the tops of their voices, they started on a frantic run up through the woods.

The piling was rough and slippery at the same time. The minutes passed, each seeming an hour to the dripping lily maid. Why didn't somebody come? Suppose they had fainted, one and all? Suppose nobody ever came? Suppose she grew so tired and cramped that she could hold on no longer? Anne looked at the wicked green depths below her, wavering with long, oily shadows and shivered. Her imagination began to suggest all manner of gruesome possibilities.

Then, just as she thought she really could not endure the ache in her arms and wrists another moment, Gilbert Blythe came rowing under the bridge in Harmon Andrews' dory.

Gilbert glanced up. To his amazement he beheld a white face looking down at him with big frightened eyes.

"Anne Shirley! What in heck are you doing?" he exclaimed.

Anne couldn't help herself. "Fishing for lake trout," she snapped.

Without another word, Gilbert helped her into the dory.

"We were playing Elaine," began Anne, so embarrassed she could hardly bring herself to look at her rescuer, "and I had to drift down to Camelot in the barge . . . I mean the dory. The dory sprang a leak and I had to climb onto the piling or sink. Now please be good enough to row me ashore."

Although vastly amused, Gilbert made no comment. He merely did as he was asked and rowed her to the landing. Refusing his assistance, Anne sprang quickly to shore.

But Gilbert was equally quick. Jumping out of the dory, he laid a detaining hand on her arm. "Wait a minute, Anne!" he said hurriedly, "I was just over at the Post Office to see if the exam results had been published and . . . ."

"Congratulations on coming first, Gilbert!" interrupted Anne with a toss of her dripping hair. "I'm sure you're very proud of your achievement."

Gilbert stared at her. "We tied for first place, you ninny. You and I." He glanced at the ground. "I figured *you'd* have it for sure."

Anne stared at him, unable to believe what she was hearing. "First? Out of all two hundred?"

Gilbert smiled ruefully. "I'm sorry you have to share it with me."

"I never expected to beat you," replied Anne honestly.

For a moment they stared at each other. Anne felt her heart give a quick, queer little beat. Under all her wounded dignity she was dimly aware that the half-shy, half-eager expression in Gilbert's hazel eyes was something that was very good to see.

"Can't we be friends, Anne?" he said slowly. "I'm sorry I ever said anything about your hair. It was so long ago. Aren't you ever going to forgive me."

That scene of two years before flashed vividly through Anne's mind. Once again Gilbert's teasing voice, his cry of "Carrots!" rang in her ears. Once again she saw herself disgraced before the whole school. Her softening determination stiffened. "You hurt my feelings excruciatingly," she heard herself say. Her voice sounded cold.

"Can't we be friends, Anne?"

"I only said it because I wanted to meet you so much," Gilbert admitted. "Look, c'mon, Anne; why can't we be friends?"

But Anne had turned on her heel. "Why can't you figure it out, if you're so clever, Gilbert Blythe?" she retorted, as she ran off up the hill.

She held her head very high as she ran, but she was conscious of a powerful feeling of regret. Why couldn't she have answered Gilbert differently? Of course he had hurt her feelings terribly, but still . . . . Altogether Anne felt as if it would be a relief to sit down and have a good cry. She was shaking, for the reaction from her fright and cramped clinging was beginning to make itself felt.

Halfway home, she met Jane and Diana rushing back to the pond in a state near frenzy. Behind them came Matthew, and in the distance Anne could see Marilla, followed by a bustling Mrs. Rachel. They had all been alerted by the terrified girls.

"Oh Anne," gasped Diana, fairly falling on Anne's neck and weeping with relief and delight, "Oh, Anne . . . we thought . . . you were . . . drowned . . . and we felt like murderers . . . because we had made . . . you be . . . Elaine. And Ruby is in hysterics . . . . Oh, Anne, how did you escape!"

"I climbed up on one of the piles," explained Anne wearily, "and Gilbert Blythe came along and rowed me to shore."

"Oh, how romantic, Anne!" breathed Jane ecstatically. "Of course you'll speak to him from now on?"

"Of course I will not!" flashed Anne, "And I don't ever want to hear the word 'romance' again, Jane Andrews!"

At that moment, Marilla caught up to the little group. When Diana had come dashing toward her, sobbing out the news that Anne had drowned, Marilla had had a revelation. In the sudden stab of fear that pierced her to the heart, she had realized just how much Anne had come to mean to her. Now she folded the wet girl in her arms.

"When are you ever going to learn sense, child?" was all she said.

Anne smiled up at her. "I think my prospects are brightening," she replied, taking heart from Marilla's embrace, "I just heard the results from Queen's. Gilbert Blythe and I tied for first place."

Everybody tried to speak at once. Matthew and Marilla simply beamed with pride. "I must say you've done pretty well for yourself, Anne," allowed Marilla, trying to hide her extreme delight in Anne from Mrs. Rachel's critical eye. But that good soul spoke up heartily.

"I guess she has done well, Marilla," she said. "Far be it from me to be backward when praise is due. You're a credit to us all, Anne Shirley, and we're proud of you!"

Anne gazed at the smiling faces of the people she had grown to love. "I'm simply dazzled inside," she admitted, "I want to say a hundred things, but I can't find the words."

The idea that their Anne could ever be at a loss for words, made them all laugh as they wound their way homeward.

For Anne, the summer days slipped by like golden beads on the necklace of the year. And suddenly, September had come around again, yellow and glowing. But this time Anne would not be returning to the small, safe world of Avonlea school. She was going to Queen's. She was going to study to become a teacher. She was going to have to leave Matthew and Marilla.

As the train drew into Bright River station, Matthew reached for Anne's bag. But Anne forestalled him. "I'll take it, Matthew," she said, "It'll be easier if I go quickly by myself."

Marilla's eyes were suspiciously bright. "Humph," was her only comment, "let's not get emotional over nothing."

Anne put down her bag. "Nothing!" she exclaimed, "Why you and Matthew mean everything to me." Reaching over, she leaned her soft cheek fondly against Marilla's lined one.

Marilla fought back her tears. "All this foolishness," she said hoarsely, nodding in Matthew's direction, "I guess you may as well kiss him, too."

"That wasn't luck. That was Providence. He knew we needed her."

Anne kissed Matthew tenderly, then climbed quickly onto the train.

"I'm afraid for her, Matthew," said Marilla, as the train pulled away from the platform. "She'll be gone so long. She'll get terrible lonesome."

"You mean *we'll* get terrible lonesome," Matthew replied, putting his arm about his sister's shoulder. He took a deep breath and blinked rapidly once or twice. "Well now . . .," he said, "that Mrs. Spencer, sure made a lucky mistake, all them years ago."

"That wasn't luck. That was Providence," said Marilla emphatically, and this time she made no attempt to hide the tears starting into her eyes. "He knew we needed her."

Anne's train arrived in Charlottetown just in time for her to attend the opening of the Academy. What with meeting all the new students, learning to know the professors by sight, and being organized into classes, her first day sped by in a whirl of excitement.

Miss Stacey's entire class had passed the entrance examination to the teacher's college. Most of them had elected to take the regular course. This meant they would spend two years studying before obtaining a teaching certificate. Only Anne and Gilbert, on Miss Stacey's advice, had chosen to try for a First Class teacher's licence in one year.

Anne was conscious of a pang of loneliness when she found herself in a room with fifty other students, not one of whom she knew, except the tall, brown-haired boy across the room. Knowing him in the way she did, was not going to help her much in terms of friendship, she reflected. Yet she was glad they were to be in the same class, for the old rivalry could still be carried on. Indeed, Anne would hardly have known what to do if it had been lacking.

"Gilbert looks awfully determined," she thought to herself, "I suppose he's making up his mind here and now to win the gold medal at the end of the year. What a splendid chin he has! To think I never noticed it before."

It was the first time Anne had ever been away from Matthew and Marilla for more than one night. Most of the other girls had relatives in town, with whom they could live. Diana's Aunt Josephine had offered to take Anne, but her house was so far from the Academy that it was out of the question. So Miss Barry had hunted up a boarding house, assuring Matthew and Marilla that it was the very place for Anne.

Looking about her narrow little room, with its empty bookcase and pictureless walls, Anne couldn't help but long for her own cozy room at Green Gables. A horrible choke came into her throat as she thought of Matthew and Marilla sitting by the fire in the kitchen, and the light from Diana's window shining out through the gap in the trees.

In the agony of homesickness that seized her during those first few weeks, she thought frequently of Gilbert and the friendship she had so scornfully refused. She could not help imagining that it would be very pleasant to have such a friend as Gilbert to jest and chatter with and exchange ideas about books and studies and ambitions. The thought of such companionship so appealed to her that one night she sat down and wrote him a letter. In it she apologized for her rudeness to him and wondered politely whether from now on they could be friends.

The next morning, feeling her courage already slipping, she hurried down to the men's residence at Queen's, planning to leave the letter with the hall porter. But instead of accepting the letter, the hall porter motioned Anne to the sitting-room, where, he said, she would find Mr. Blythe in person.

Flustered, and with her heart thumping in the most uncalled-for manner, Anne approached the sitting room. There Gilbert stood, his back to the door, his elbow resting on the piano. He was gazing admiringly, or so Anne interpreted from her reading of his back, at the person seated on the piano stool. From this person's profile, Anne was also able to read volumes. She was raven-haired. She was winsome. That she was also intelligent there could be no doubt. For even as Anne quietly entered the room, she was describing in clear, carrying tones, how she intended to carry off the Avery scholarship.

"Can't you just picture it, Gilbert?" she laughed, and her long, slender fingers picked out a triumphal march on the piano keys, "Emily Clay, winner of the Avery!"

For one long moment, Anne stood frozen in the doorway. Then she turned and fled.

As she stormed back across the quadrangle, scattering little white flecks of ripped letter in her wake, Anne was torn between tears and fury. The Avery scholarship was one of the most prestigious scholarships in the Maritime Provinces. It meant two hundred and fifty dollars a year for four years at Redmond College. It meant a good university degree, and a chance to make Matthew and Marilla proud of her. Besides, it was awarded for distinction in English, a field that Anne regarded as uniquely her own. Who did this Emily Clay think she was, anyway. Setting her cap at the Avery? And at Gilbert too, for that matter. Well, she'd reckoned without Anne Shirley.

Gradually, Anne's homesickness wore off. She wrote long, devoted letters to Marilla and Matthew. During the autumn and early winter, she made several weekend visits home, which helped a great deal. Gradually too, she drew a little circle of friends around her at Queen's. But after the Christmas holidays, she threw herself into her work with even more than her customary enthusiasm and concentration. So hard did she work that by early summer, when the examination results were due out, she barely had enough energy left to care what they might be. Or at least, so she claimed to her friend, Jane Andrews. The final results of all the examinations were to be posted that morning on the bulletin board at the college and Anne and Jane were walking down the street toward campus together.

"You'll just have to read the announcements and then come and tell me, Jane," Anne decided, "and in the name of our long friendship, I implore you to do it as quickly as possible. If I have failed, just say so, without trying to break it gently. And whatever you do, don't sympathize with me. Promise me this?"

But Jane's solemn promises were interrupted by the loud cheers of boys streaming down the steps from the hall where the results were posted. On their shoulders they carried Gilbert Blythe.

"Hurrah!" they were yelling at the tops of their voices, "Hurrah for Gilbert Blythe, Medalist!"

For a moment Anne felt one sickening pang of defeat and disappointment. So she had failed and Gilbert had won! And then! Somebody called out: "Three cheers for Anne Shirley, winner of the Avery!" Then Anne too was the centre of a laughing, congratulating group. Her shoulders were thumped, her hands shaken vigorously. She was pulled and pushed and hugged. Through it all, her one thought was of Matthew and Marilla, and how proud this news would make them. Strangely enough, of Emily Clay she thought not at all.

Commencement was the next important happening. The graduation ceremony was held in the big assembly hall of the Academy. Speeches were made, essays read, songs sung, and diplomas, prizes, and medals awarded. Matthew and Marilla attended the ceremony. They had eyes and ears for only one student on the platform—a tall girl in palest green, with faintly flushed cheeks and starry eyes. It was that same girl—their girl—who read the best essay and was pointed out and whispered about as the Avery winner.

"Reckon you're glad we kept her, Marilla? whispered Matthew, when Anne had finished her essay.

"It's not the first time I've been glad," retorted Marilla. "You do like to rub things in, Matthew Cuthbert."

Anne went home to Avonlea with Matthew and Marilla that evening. The apple blossoms were out and the world was fresh and young. In her own white room, where Marilla had set a flowering house rose on the window sill, Anne looked about her and drew a long breath of happiness. She was back at Green Gables at last, with three golden months of vacation stretching before her.

The very next afternoon, Anne and Diana set off for a long

"Three cheers for Anne Shirley, winner of the Avery!"

stroll along the old birch path by the sea. Arm in arm, they talked and wandered until the sun was setting and the glimmering sea was streaked with long shivers of pink. Anne sighed in sheer contentment. "Oh, Diana, isn't that breath of mint delicious? I can't bear the thought of leaving here again."

"Four years," murmured Diana in dismay, "I'll probably be old and grey by the time you come back from university."

"More likely you'll be married to a dashingly handsome young man and much too busy with babies to be interested in your former bosom friend," laughed Anne.

"Such as who?" wondered Diana gaily, "Moody Spurgeon, perhaps?"

"I'll pray that someone wonderful comes to Avonlea and sweeps you off your feet," Anne promised.

Diana's smile faded. "Gilbert Blythe is getting Avonlea school, Anne."

Anne felt a sudden little sensation of dismayed surprise. She had expected Gilbert would be going to college, too—just like herself.

"His father can't afford to send him to Redmond," Diana was saying. "He's going to have to earn his way by teaching."

Anne wondered what she would do without their inspiring rivalry. She was afraid everything, even studying for a real degree, would seem flat without her friend the enemy. "I wish him luck," she said finally. "He's a talented and determined young man."

Diana's expression was odd. "You mean . . . ." She hesitated, looking down at the daisy she was holding. "Do you mean that as far as you're concerned, he's fair game?"

Anne stared at her friend in astonishment. "Why Diana Barry! If you were interested in Gilbert Blythe why on earth didn't you ever say so?"

"Because I thought my bosom friend was in love with him," replied Diana quietly.

It came to Anne then that she was not the only person who had grown up in the past year. Almost shyly she reached over

"Goodnight, sweet Diana."

and kissed Diana on the cheek.

"Goodnight, sweet Diana," she said, before turning back toward Green Gables.

Diana returned her smile. "Goodnight Anne," she replied affectionately.

The following evening, Anne went with Matthew to fetch the cows from the back pasture. The woods were all gloried through with sunset and the warm splendour of it streamed down through the hill gaps in the west. Anne's thoughts were absorbed in the beauty of the twilight. Behind her she could hear Matthew urging on Buttercup, who always dallied. Suddenly, he gave a stifled cry and a gasp. Anne looked back. Matthew had fallen to the ground. She flew to his side.

"What . . . is . . . it? What . . . is . . . it, Matthew?" she cried, alarm in every jerky word. He lay still. Dropping to her knees, she gathered his head onto her lap. His face was strangely drawn and gray.

"Matthew . . . Please Matthew . . . " She felt helpless, bewildered. "I'll go get the doctor . . . Matthew . . . "

He opened his eyes. They were the same calm, reassuring blue they had always been. But his voice seemed to come from far away. "Well now . . . " he muttered. He sounded faintly surprised. "I . . . got old . . . and never noticed . . . I worked hard . . . all . . . my life . . . I'd rather drop . . . in harness . . . "

Anne bent her head toward his. Gently she smoothed the grey hair back from his forehead. "If I'd been the boy you sent for, I could have spared you in so many ways," she said wistfully.

He smiled his shy smile at her. She knew every line in the kind face.

"I never wanted a boy . . . I only wanted you, from that first day," he whispered. "Don't ever change, Anne. . . . I love my little girl . . . I'm so proud of my little girl . . . " His eyes closed.

"Matthew . . . " pleaded Anne urgently, "Matthew, don't . . . "

But the breath had gone from his body. Anne gazed down at the still face, the face that for her meant home and comfort and love. For a long time she knelt there in the long grass, cradling Matthew's body in her arms.

Two days afterward, they carried Matthew Cuthbert over his homestead threshold, away from the fields he had tilled, the orchards he had loved, and the trees he had planted. They carried him to the graveyard, where the mother he had cared for so tenderly was buried.

All of Avonlea turned out for the funeral. For the first time shy, quiet Matthew Cuthbert was a person of central importance; the white majesty of death had fallen on him and set him apart as one crowned.

Anne stood by his graveside, her tearless eyes burning in her white face, a dull, throbbing pain aching inside her. People who had loved Matthew wept unashamedly. After the funeral, they came up to Marilla and Anne, pressing their hands, murmuring words of sympathy. But to Anne it seemed as if she stood outside them all, with only the dull ache for company. Sometimes, it seemed as if Matthew couldn't be dead. Sometimes, as if he had been dead for a long, long time. She longed to be quiet and alone. Perhaps then her tears for Matthew would come.

As they left the graveyard, Gilbert stepped forward out of the shadow of the trees. He held his hat in his hands. "Miss Cuthbert, Anne . . . . " He looked at each directly, "I'm very sorry for your loss."

Marilla's eyes were brimming over with tears. She held them back with difficulty. "Thank you, Gilbert Blythe," she said simply.

Anne too wanted to thank him. She felt drawn toward his directness and honesty. But she was locked inside herself. Her eyes glanced up at him for the briefest of seconds. Then taking Marilla's arm, she walked slowly out of the cemetery.

In the night, Anne awakened, with the stillness and darkness about her. The recollection of the past few days came over her like a wave of sorrow. She could see Matthew's face smiling at her as he had smiled that last time. She could hear his voice saying, "My girl . . . I love my little girl." Then at last the tears came and Anne wept her heart out. Marilla heard her and crept in to comfort her.

"There now," she murmured, holding Anne closely, "Crying won't bring him back."

Anne's voice was choked with sobs. "Let me cry, Marilla. The tears don't hurt like that ache did. Keep your arm around me, just for a little while."

Marilla rocked her like a child. "I don't know what I'd do if you weren't here . . . if you'd never come," she whispered into Anne's hair. "I know I've been strict with you; but you mustn't think I don't love you as much as Matthew did. It's never been easy for me to say things out of my heart, but I love you as dear as if you were my own flesh and blood . . . There, there . . ." For the sobs seemed to increase slightly, "It isn't right to cry so, God knows best."

"Oh, Marilla," Anne raised her tear-stained face, "Marilla, what will we do without him?"

Marilla shook her head wordlessly. Tears rolled slowly down her cheeks. "He was always such a good, kind brother to me," she mourned.

This time Anne put her arms around Marilla, "We have each other now," she reminded her gently.

Always there was that aching sense of loss. But even at Green Gables, affairs slipped into their old groove and work was done and duties fulfilled with regularity as before.

Then one afternoon, Anne happened to glance out a front window. Marilla was in the yard, talking to John Sadler from Carmody. Anne wondered what he could have been saying to bring that look to Marilla's face.

"What did Mr. Sadler want, Marilla?" she asked, hurrying outside.

Marilla fiddled with her apron. She was careful not to look at Anne. "He once offered to buy Green Gables, and he's still interested."

"He was always such a good, kind brother to me."

Anne wondered if she had heard correctly. "Buy Green Gables! Marilla!"

This time Marilla looked straight at Anne. "Anne, I don't know what else to do. My eyes are getting worse. Dr. Spencer says if my headaches persist I may lose my sight completely. What if I can't run this place?" Again she looked away. "Rachel has kindly offered to let me live with her and Thomas."

Anne still couldn't believe her ears. "But you can't sell Green Gables!"

Marilla's worn face was creased with anxiety. "I'd go crazy if there was trouble and I was all alone here. I'm sorry that you won't have a home to come to on your vacations." Her eyes scanned the old place, taking in every loved, familiar detail. "I never thought I'd see the day when I'd have to sell it, but we'll survive, somehow."

Anne squared her shoulders. Now was as good a time as any to break the news. "You won't have to stay here alone, Marilla," she said resolutely, "I'm not going to Redmond."

This time it was Marilla's turn to express amazement. "Not going to Redmond?" she repeated blankly, "Why, what do you mean?"

"I'm not going to take that scholarship," Anne explained. "I'd already decided, but I hadn't told you yet. Mr. Barry has promised to rent our fields next year, and I'm going to take the school at Carmody. They need a teacher there."

"Carmody's miles away," objected Marilla.

Anne ignored the interruption. "I can drive back and forth until the weather gets bad. Then I'll board and come home on weekends."

Marilla shook her head. "I won't let you sacrifice your education for me. I won't allow it, Anne Shirley."

Anne grinned suddenly. "Marilla Cuthbert, I am *going* to do it. I am sixteen years old and just as stubborn as you are. So there."

Marilla's smile lit up the whole of Green Gables. "You blessed girl!" she laughed, giving in, "I know I ought to stick to it and make you go to college. But I know I can't, so I won't try. I'll make it up to you, though," she added, as she hugged Anne closely.

Strolling back into the house together, Marilla looked affectionately at the slender girl by her side.

"Gilbert Blythe will be teaching, too, won't he?" she asked suddenly.

Anne nodded. "Yes," she said briefly, "I understand the trustees have promised Avonlea school to him."

"What a nice looking young fellow he is," mused Marilla. "He looks a lot like his father did at that age. We used to be real good friends, he and I." She glanced over at Anne. "People called him my beau."

Anne looked up with swift interest. "What happened? Why didn't you . . . ?"

"We had a quarrel. I wouldn't forgive him when he asked me to. I wanted to, after a while . . . but I was stubborn and I wanted to punish him first." Marilla shook her head slowly. "He never came back. I always felt rather sorry. I've always kind of wished I'd forgiven him when I had the chance."

"So you've had a bit of romance in your life, too," said Anne softly.

Marilla smiled. "I suppose you might call it that. You wouldn't think so to look at me, would you? But you never can tell about people from their outsides, now can you?"

When it became known in Avonlea that Anne Shirley had given up the idea of going to college and intended to stay home and teach, there was a good deal of discussion over it. Most of the good folks, not knowing about Marilla's eyes, thought she was foolish. Mrs. Lynde did not. She came up one evening and found Anne and Marilla sitting on the front porch in the warm, scented summer dusk. They liked to sit there when the twilight came down and the white moths flew about in the garden and the odor of mint filled the air.

"I'm glad to hear you've given up your notion of going to college, Anne," she announced, depositing her substantial person on a protesting wicker rocker. "I don't believe in girls going to college with the men and cramming their heads full of Latin and Greek and all that nonsense."

"But I'll be taking my courses by correspondence, just the same." replied Anne, laughing.

Mrs. Rachel lifted her hands in holy horror. "With all the

work you'll have to do, teaching over at Carmody, and looking after Green Gables? . . . Marilla!" she commanded sharply, "talk some sense into that girl."

"Oh mind your own business for once, Rachel, and leave her alone," retorted Marilla crisply. "You know Anne thrives on studying."

Anne left them to their amiable bickering and wandered down the long hill that sloped to the Lake of Shining Waters. It was past sunset now and all Avonlea lay before her in a dreamlike afterlight. How greatly things had changed since she had returned from Queen's so full of hope and ambition and gladness!

It had been shortly after Matthew's death that Anne had first realized that Marilla's eyesight was in danger. That same evening, she had sat by her bedroom window, alone with her tears and her heaviness of heart. It had been a hard decision to make. But she had looked her duty frankly in the face and found it a friend. Before she went to bed, there was a smile on her lips and peace in her heart. Now, as she felt the freshness of the wind against her cheek, a wind that had blown over honey-sweet fields of clover, she felt no regret for Redmond College. She knew her decision to stay had been the right one.

Halfway down the hill she saw a figure approaching her on horseback. It was Gilbert Blythe.

"Miss Cuthbert said I would probably find you here," he said, dismounting and holding out a letter.

Mystified, Anne read the letter. It took her a while to grasp its meaning. For the letter agreed formally to a suggestion put forward by Gilbert Blythe that Anne Shirley be engaged to teach at Avonlea Public School.

"I took the liberty of speaking to the trustees about an exchange," Gilbert explained. "I'll be getting Carmody and you can stay at Green Gables."

He took Anne's breath away. "I . . . I don't know what to say," she stammered.

He smiled. "Don't say anything."

"But you'll have to pay for your board. You'll never save enough for college! No, I can't let you . . . . "

"I'll save enough," replied Gilbert steadily. "Besides, I'll keep up with my studies by correspondence."

"Why, that's what I'm doing too!" exclaimed Anne in surprise. She held out her hand to him. "Gilbert," she said, her cheeks slowly flushing scarlet, "Thank you for giving up the school for me. It was very good of you . . . and I want you to know that I appreciate it."

Gilbert took the offered hand readily. "I figure you can give me some coaching and we'll call it a fair exchange."

Anne laughed and tried unsuccessfully to withdraw her hand.

"Aren't you afraid I might break another slate over your head?" she asked shyly.

He reached out and gently touched an auburn curl, which the wind had set dancing. "I'm more worried I might break one over yours," he grinned. Then taking his horse's reins in one hand, he put his other arm around Anne's shoulder. "C'mon carrots," he said teasingly, "I'll walk you home."

Marilla looked curiously at Anne when she entered the kitchen.

"Who was that came up the lane with you, Anne?"

"Gilbert Blythe," answered Anne, vexed to find herself blushing yet again.

"I didn't think you and Gilbert Blythe were such good friends that you'd stand for half an hour at the gate talking to him," said Marilla with a slow smile.

"We haven't been . . . we've been good enemies. But we've decided to be good friends in future. Were we really there half an hour?"

There was a teasing gleam in Marilla's eye. "I've never known that clock to lie. Not since Matthew brought it home from Carmody."

"It seemed just a few minutes. But you see, we've years of lost conversations to catch up with, Marilla."

Anne sat long at her window that night, companioned by a glad content. The stars twinkled over the pointed firs in the hollow and the wind purred softly in the cherry boughs.

Her horizons had closed in since the night of Matthew's death. But if the path set before her feet was to be narrow, she knew that flowers of quiet happiness would bloom along it. Nothing could rob her of her birthright of fancy or her ideal world of dreams.

" 'God's in His heaven,' " whispered Anne softly, " 'all's right with the world.' "